U0079310

Travel

旅遊

英文
一點通

國家圖書館出版品預行編目資料

旅遊英文一點通 / 鍾季霖著

-- 初版. -- 新北市：雅典文化，民110.09

面；　公分. --（全民學英文；61）

ISBN 978-986-06463-9-9(平裝)

1. 英語　2. 旅遊　3. 會話

805.188 110013240

全民學英文系列 61

旅遊英文一點通

著／鍾季霖

責任編輯／鍾季霖

美術編輯／鄭孝儀

封面設計／林鈺恆

法律顧問：方圓法律事務所／涂成樞律師

總經銷：永續圖書有限公司

永續圖書線上購物網
www.foreverbooks.com.tw

出版日／2021年09月

ⓐ 雅典文化

出版社

22103　新北市汐止區大同路三段194號9樓之1

TEL　(02) 8647-3663

FAX　(02) 8647-3660

交際篇

機場篇

Part 3 交通工具篇

Part 4　當地生活篇

Part 5　飲食篇

購物篇

觀光篇

休閒娛樂篇

辦公室篇

Part 10 就醫篇

★ 基本學習

KK 音標總表

母音篇

音標	發音要訣	例字
[i]	發音類似注音符號「一」，尾音拉長，是長母音	seat
[ɪ]	念起來也是"一"，但是是短母音	sit
[e]	發音類似注音的"ㄟ一"，是長母音	pain
[ɛ]	發音類似注音的"ㄝ"，發音短促，嘴巴半開，是短母音	met
[æ]	把嘴巴張成「啊」的形，但唸「ㄝ」的聲音	mat
[ɑ]	發音類似注音符號「ㄚ」，嘴巴張大，尾音稍微拉長，是長母音	hot
[o]	發音類似注音符號「ㄡ」，嘴巴打開後慢慢收回，尾音拉長，是長母音	boat
[ɔ]	發音類似注音符號「ㄛ」，嘴巴張成大圓形，是短母音	dog
[u]	發音類似注音符號「ㄨ」，嘴巴嘟起來，尾音拉長，是長母音	too
[ʊ]	發音類似注音符號「ㄨ」，嘴巴微張，用發「ㄜ」音的位置發「ㄨ」，是短母音	put
[ʌ]	發音類似注音符號「ㄜ」與「ㄚ」之間，稍微偏向「ㄚ」音，是短母音	cut
[ə]	發音類似注音符號「ㄜ」，是弱化音	again

音標	發音要訣	例字
[ɚ]	發音類似注音符號「ㄦ」，捲舌音出現在輕音節	father
[ɝ]	發音類似注音符號「ㄦ」，捲舌音出現在重音節	bird
[aɪ]	發音類似注音符號「ㄞ」，雙母音	pie
[aʊ]	發音類似注音符號「ㄠ」，雙母音	house
[ɔɪ]	發音類似注音符號「ㄛㄧ」，雙母音	coin

子音篇

無聲子音

音標	發音要訣	例字
[p]	發音類似注音符號「ㄆ」	pet
[t]	發音類似注音符號「ㄊ」	ten
[k]	發音類似注音符號「ㄎ」	kite
[f]	發音類似注音符號「ㄈ」，聲帶不振動	fine
[s]	發音類似注音符號「ㄙ」，聲帶不振動	see
[θ]	舌尖放在上下排牙齒中間，輕輕咬住，吹氣	thank
[ʃ]	發音類似注音符號「ㄒㄩ」	shy
[tʃ]	發音類似「ㄑㄩ」	chair
[h]	發音類似注音符號「ㄏ」	hello

基本學習

有聲子音

音標	發音要訣	例字
[b]	發音類似注音符號「ㄅ」	book
[d]	發音類似注音符號「ㄉ」	day
[g]	發音類似注音符號「ㄍ」	good
[v]	上排牙齒輕咬下嘴唇，再吹氣，同時振動聲帶	voice
[z]	用 [s] 的位置發音，發成有聲	zoo
[ð]	舌尖放在上下排牙齒中間，輕輕咬住，吹氣的同時振動聲帶	breathe
[ʒ]	用 [ʃ] 的位置發音，發成有聲	measure
[dʒ]	母音前，與母音拼音，發音類似「居 + ㄜ」；不與母音拼音或字尾時，發音類似「ㄐㄩ」	joke；judge
[l]	母音前，發音類似「ㄌㄜ」；不與母音拼音或在字尾，發音類似「ㄡ」	lie；bell
[r]	放母音前，發音類似「ㄖㄨㄜ」；放母音後，發音類似「ㄦ」	rice；dare
[m]	發音類似注音符號「ㄇ」	mom
[n]	發音類似注音符號「ㄋ」	nice
[ŋ]	發音類似注音符號「ㄥ」，後舌碰到上顎	sing
[j]	發音類似注音符號「ㄧㄜ」	yes
[w]	發音類似注音符號「ㄨㄜ」	we

旅遊英文一點通

🎧 track 03

相關單字、片語

one	一
two	二
three	三
four	四
five	五
six	六
seven	七
eight	八
nine	九
ten	十
eleven	十一
twelve	十二
thirteen	十三
fourteen	十四
fifteen	十五
sixteen	十六
seventeen	十七
eighteen	十八
nineteen	十九
twenty	二十
twenty-one	二十一
thirty	三十
forty	四十
fifty	五十
sixty	六十

014

seventy	七十
eighty	八十
ninety	九十
hundred	百
thousand	千
hundred thousand	十萬
million	百萬
billion	十億
trillion	兆

序數

first	第一；第一的
second	第二；第二的
third	第三；第三的
fourth	第四；第四的
fifth	第五；第五的
sixth	第六；第六的
seventh	第七；第七的
eighth	第八；第八的
ninth	第九；第九的
tenth	第十；第十的

星期

Monday	星期一
Tuesday	星期二
Wednesday	星期三

Thursday	星期四
Friday	星期五
Saturday	星期六
Sunday	星期日

| 月份 |
January	一月
February	二月
March	三月
April	四月
May	五月
June	六月
July	七月
August	八月
September	九月
October	十月
November	十一月
December	十二月

| 季節 |
spring	春天
summer	夏天
fall / autumn	秋天
winter	冬天

顏色	
red	紅色
pink	粉紅色
orange	橙色
yellow	黃色
brown	棕色
green	綠色
blue	藍色
purple	紫色
white	白色
black	黑色
silver	銀色
gold	金色

1

交際篇

自我介紹

會話實例

A Hi, my name is John. What's your name?

嗨,我叫約翰,你叫什麼名字?

B My name is Rebecca, you can call me Becky.

我叫蕾貝卡,你可以叫我貝琪。

A Nice to meet you!

很高興認識你!

B Nice to meet you, too.

我也是,很高興認識你。

A We just moved here from downtown last week.

我們上星期才從市區搬過來這裡。

B Welcome to the neighborhood! Let me know if you need any help. My husband and I will be glad to help.

歡迎來到這裡!若是有需要任何幫忙都可以跟我說,我和先生很樂意幫忙。

① 交際篇

Ⓐ Sure, thank you!
好的，謝謝！

延伸例句

▶ What's your name?
你叫什麼名字？

▶ My name is…
我叫做...

▶ You can call me…
請稱呼我...就可以了。

▶ Nice to meet you.
很高興認識你。

相關單字、片語

surname [ˋsɚˏnem]	姓氏
nickname [ˋnɪkˏnem]	綽號
meet [mit]	遇見；碰上；認識
downtown [ˏdaʊnˋtaʊn]	城市商業區
neighborhood [ˋnebɚˏhʊd]	鄰近地區
glad [glæd]	高興的

1.2 打招呼

會話實例

Ⓐ Hi! How are you?

嗨！你好嗎？

Ⓑ I'm fine, I just came back from my vacation. How about you?

我很好，我剛放完假回來。你呢？

Ⓐ I'm good, thank you.

我很好，謝謝。

Ⓑ How's your family?

你家人好嗎？

Ⓐ They're good. My daughter is having her graduation next week.

他們很好，我女兒下禮拜要畢業了。

Ⓑ Oh that's great! Congratulations!

喔太棒了！恭喜你！

Ⓐ Thank you!

謝謝！

延伸例句

「你好嗎」的其他問法：

▶ What's up?
最近在忙什麼？(口語的用法)

▶ How are you doing?
你好嗎？

▶ How's it going?
你過得如何？

▶ How's everything?
一切安好？

▶ How's life treating you?
最近日子過得如何呀？

▶ How have you been?
你過得如何？（適用於一陣子沒見的對象）

答覆的方式：

▶ Wonderful.
好極了。

▶ Great.
很棒。

▶ Pretty good.
很棒。

▶ Not bad.
還不錯。

▶ I'm doing ok.
還不錯。

▶ As usual.
還好。

▶ So so.
普普通通。

▶ Not so good.
不太好。

▶ Awful.
很糟。

相關單字、片語

fine [faɪn]	美好的；傑出的；纖細的
graduation [ˌgrædʒʊˋeʃən]	畢業典禮
Congratulations [kənˌgrætʃəˋleʃənz]	
	祝賀；恭喜
treat [trit]	對待；看待；處理
See you later	等會見

1.3 道早安

會話實例

A Good morning, Mrs. Yang.
早安,楊太太。

B Good morning, William.
早安,威廉。

A Where are you going?
您要去哪裡?

B I'm going to church.
我要去教堂。

A Please say hello to Mr. Davis for me.
請幫我跟戴維斯先生問好

B Will do.
我會的。

A Have a nice day!
祝您有個美好的一天!

B You, too.
你也是。

延伸例句

▶ Where are you going?
  你要去哪裡？

▶ Where are you headed?
  你要去哪裡？

▶ I'm going to the beach.
  我要去海邊。

相關單字、片語

Have a nice day	祝你有個美好的一天
Have fun	祝你玩得開心
Good morning	早安
Good afternoon	午安
Good evening	晚上好
Good night	晚安
Sweet dream	祝你好夢
Sleep tight	睡個安穩的覺；晚安

track 08

1.4 你從哪裡來

會話實例

Ⓐ Where are you from?

你是哪裡人？

Ⓑ I'm from Turkey. What about you?

我是土耳其人，你呢？

Ⓐ My parents are both from Taiwan, but I was born and raised in Canada.

我的父母都是台灣人，但我在加拿大出生、長大。

Ⓑ Which city?

哪個城市？

Ⓐ Vancouver. I'm currently working in Singapore after my studies in the UK.

溫哥華。我在英國念完書後，現在在新加坡工作。

Ⓑ You're a real cosmopolitan.

你真是四海為家。

Ⓐ haha, yea.

哈哈，對呀。

延伸例句

▶ Where do you come from?
你從哪裡來？

▶ Which city are you from?
你從哪個城市來？

▶ I was raised in the capital of Nigeria, Abuja.
我在奈及利亞的首都—阿不加—長大。

▶ I grew up in Tainan City.
我在台南市長大。

▶ I studied in New York.
我在紐約念書。

相關單字、片語

born [bɔrn]	出生的；天生的
raise [rez]	養育、照顧；舉起；增加
grow up	長大
study [ˋstʌdɪ]	學習
cosmopolitan [ˌkɑzməˋpɑlətn]	
	世界性的；四海為家的

track 09

1.5 問歲數

會話實例

Ⓐ How old are you?

你幾歲？

Ⓑ I'm turning 18 years old next week.

我下週要滿十八歲了。

Ⓐ How do you feel?

你感覺如何？

Ⓑ I'm excited.

我很興奮。

Ⓐ Great. Any plans?

太棒了，你有任何計畫嗎？

Ⓑ Yea, we're going to the Stars n Bars, wanna join?

有，我們要去星星酒吧，你要一起來嗎？

Ⓐ Sure!

好呀！

延伸例句

▶ How old is he / she?
他/她幾歲？

▶ He / she is 17 years old.
他/她十七歲。

▶ Ben is a seven-year-old boy.
班是個七歲的男孩。

▶ She's one year old.
她今年一歲。

▶ Martin is at the age of thirteen.
馬丁十三歲。

▶ My dad turned 60 years old yesterday.
我爸爸昨天滿六十歲。

▶ When is your birthday?
你生日是幾月幾號？

▶ My birthday is July 5.
我生日是七月五號。

相關單字、片語

excited [ɪk`saɪtɪd]	興奮的
age [edʒ]	年齡
數字-year-old ...	...歲的
at the age of	某人...歲
birthday [`bɝˌθde]	生日

track 10

1.6

道歉

會話實例

A Hey, have you seen my cup on the table?
嘿，你有看到我放在桌上的杯子嗎？

B You mean the green one?
你是指綠色的那個杯子？

A Yes, did you see it?
對，你有看到嗎？

B Oh my god, I threw it away yesterday.
天啊，我昨天把它丟掉了。

A Are you serious? That's a souvenir I bought in Disneyland!
你是認真的嗎？那是我從迪士尼買的紀念品耶！

B I'm really sorry.
我真的很抱歉。

A It's ok. You didn't mean it.
沒關係，你不是故意的。

B I will buy you a new one.
我會買個新的還你。

0
3
1

1 交際篇

延伸例句

▶ I am so sorry.
我很抱歉。

▶ My bad.
是我不好。

▶ It's my fault.
我的錯。

▶ I owe you an apology.
我欠你一個道歉。

▶ I sincerely apologize.
我真誠地道歉。

▶ I'm sorry for being late.
抱歉，我遲到了。

▶ I'm terribly sorry about that.
為此我感到非常抱歉。

▶ Please forgive me.
請原諒我。

▶ I really feel bad about it.
我真的感到很內疚。

▶ Sorry about the inconvenience.
對不起添麻煩了。

▶ I didn't mean to hurt your feelings.
我不是故意要讓你難過或不舒服。

▶ I'll make it up to you.
我會補償你。

▶ What can I do to make it up to you?
我要怎麼做才能補償你？

▶ He wants to make it up by spending more time with his family.
他想要藉由多花時間陪伴家人來彌補。

▶ Apology accepted.
我原諒你。

▶ I'm sorry for my careless mistake.
我對於我的疏失感到很抱歉。

▶ We forgave him for his rudeness.
我們原諒他的無禮。

▶ It's not your fault.
那不是你的錯。

相關單字、片語

throw away (ph.)	拋棄，扔掉
souvenir [`suvəˌnɪr]	紀念品
fault [fɔlt]	錯誤
owe [o]	欠

spend [spɛnd]	花（時間，精力）
apology [əˋpɑlədʒɪ]	(n.) 道歉；賠罪
apologize [əˋpɑlədʒaɪz] (v.)	道歉；認錯
to apologize for sb./sth.	為某人／某事道歉
make it up to	補償某人的損失 （或遭受的不幸、花費的錢財）
terribly [ˋtɛrəblɪ]	非常，很；可怕地
forgive [fəˋgɪv]	原諒
inconvenience [͵ɪnkənˋvinjəns]	不便；麻煩
careless [ˋkɛrlɪs]	粗心的，疏忽的；草率的； 隨便的；自然的
mistake [mɪˋstek]	錯誤，過失；誤會
rudeness [ˋrudnɪs]	無禮貌；粗野；未加工

① 交際篇

🎧 track 11

1.7

感謝

會話實例

Ⓐ Hello, we're back.

哈囉，我們回家了。

Ⓑ Hi, how was your date?

嗨，你們的約會如何？

A It was great, thank you for taking care of Amy. I really appreciate your help.

很棒，謝謝你照顧艾咪，我真的很感激你的幫忙。

B You're welcome. We had a good time. She's already asleep.

別客氣，我們玩得很開心，她已經睡著了。

A Alright, thanks again. Get home safe.

好的，再次感謝你，回家小心。

B Bye bye, see you tomorrow.

掰掰，明天見。

A See you tomorrow!

明天見！

延伸例句

▶ Thanks, John.
謝啦，約翰。

▶ Thanks a lot.
非常感謝。

▶ Thank you very much.
非常感謝你。

▶ Thank you in advance.
事先感謝你的幫助。

▶ Thank you for helping me with my homework.
感謝你幫我複習功課。

▶ Thank you for taking care of my little brother.
謝謝你照顧我弟弟。

▶ Thank you for the delicious lunch.
感謝你這一頓美味的午餐。

▶ Thank you for inviting me to dinner.
感謝你招待我吃晚餐。

▶ I'm truly grateful for your help.
我非常感激你的幫助。

▶ I would be grateful if you could send me the document.
如果你可以把文件傳給我，我會很感激你的。

▶ I'm thankful that no one was hurt in the accident.
我很感恩這次意外沒人受傷。

▶ We're so thankful that our dog survived the car accident.
我們都很感恩我們的小狗從車禍中逃過死劫。

▶ Please give your mom my thanks for the delicious pie.
幫我跟你媽媽說謝謝她美味的派。

相關單字、片語

take care of	照顧
appreciate [əˋpriʃɪͺet]	欣賞；感謝

asleep [ə`slip]	睡著的
see you tomorrow	明天見
in advance	預先
delicious [dɪ`lɪʃəs]	美味的
invite [ɪn`vaɪt]	邀請；招待
grateful [`gretfəl]	感謝的
document [`dakjəmənt]	文件
hurt [hɝt]	使受傷；使疼痛
accident [`æksədənt]	事故；災禍
survive [sə`vaɪv]	在……之後仍然生存

🎧 track 12

1.8 表達遺憾

會話實例

Ⓐ Hey, this is Kim.
嘿，我是金。

Ⓑ It's me, Beth. Thank you for the sympathy card you sent my family.
是我，貝絲。謝謝你寄給我家人的慰問卡。

Ⓐ I'm so sorry for your loss.
我對你失去親人感到遺憾。

B Thank you for your sympathy and kindness.

謝謝你的慰問與好意。

A Let me know if there's anything else I can help.

若是有需要任何幫忙，都可以讓我知道。

B Thank you. That's very thoughtful. We are grateful for friends like you at this time of sorrow.

謝謝，你真是體貼。我們很感激在這哀傷的時刻有像你這樣的朋友。

A I love you and I'm here for you.

我愛你，我會在這支持你。

延伸例句

▶ I'm sorry to hear that.
我聽到這個消息感到很遺憾。

▶ I'm so sorry to hear of your loss.
我對你失去親人感到遺憾。

▶ Please accept our deepest condolences on your grandfather's death.
請接受我們對你爺爺的去逝最真誠的哀悼。

▶ I regret to inform you that you have not been shortlisted for the interview.
　我很遺憾地通知您沒有被選上參加面試。

▶ I'm sorry to inform you that you have not passed the exam.
　我很遺憾地通知你沒有通過考試。

相關單字、片語

loss [lɔs]	喪失，損失
sympathy [ˋsɪmpəθɪ]	同情；慰問
kindness [ˋkaɪndnɪs]	仁慈；好意
sorrow [ˋsaro]	悲痛，憂傷
arrange [əˋrendʒ]	安排；籌備
grocery [ˋgrosərɪ]	食品雜貨店；食品雜貨
delivery [dɪˋlɪvərɪ]	投遞；交貨
thoughtful [ˋθɔtfəl]	體貼的，考慮周到的
condolence [kənˋdoləns]	（常複數）弔辭；弔唁；慰問
inform [ɪnˋfɔrm]	通知，告知
shortlist [ˋʃɔrtˏlɪst]	把……列入供最後挑選用的候選人名單
interview [ˋɪntɚˏvju]	面試；會見

1.9 邀請做客

會話實例

Ⓐ Hey, Woody, I was wondering if you're free this Saturday afternoon?

嘿，伍迪，我想知道你這禮拜六下午有沒有空？

Ⓑ Hey, Kevin, let me check my schedule.

嘿，凱文，我看一下我的行程。

Ⓐ We are having a yacht party.

我們要辦遊艇派對。

Ⓑ Oh, I'll be out of town on that day.

噢，我那天不在城裡。

Ⓐ Such a shame!

真可惜！

Ⓑ Thanks for inviting me though. You guys have fun!

還是謝謝你邀請我，你們好好玩！

Ⓐ Cheers!

謝啦！

❶ 交際篇

延伸例句

▶ Come over for some beers at my house.
來我家喝啤酒。

▶ I'd like to invite you to my housewarming party.
我想邀請你來我的新居派對。

▶ We will be attending.
我們會參加。

▶ I will be attending but Lily won't be able to make it.
我會到，但Lily沒法到。

▶ Sorry, we won't be able to make it.
抱歉，我們無法出席。

▶ My mother was sick and had to send her regrets.
我母親身體不適，無法出席。

▶ I've already got something on.
我有事情了。

▶ I'm afraid that I can't make it on Saturday, I'm available on Sunday though.
我這禮拜六恐怕不能出席，但我禮拜天可以。

▶ I'm so glad you could come!
我很高興你能來！

▶ It's our pleasure to have you.
很高興你能來。

▶ It's good to see you!
很高興見到你！

▶ Make yourself at home.
不要拘束，當自己家。

▶ Here are some flowers for you.
這些花送給你。

▶ Thank you for inviting us to join you and your friends.
謝謝你邀請我們加入你們和你們的朋友們。

▶ Thank you so much for the invitation.
非常感謝你的邀請。

▶ Thanks for your hospitality!
感謝熱情款待！

▶ Thank you for having me!
謝謝你的招待！

▶ What a fun time we had with you both!
我們跟你們兩個玩得很開心！

▶ We had a wonderful time at your house the other day.
我們在你家度過了很棒的時光。

旅遊英文 一點通

相關單字、片語

wonder [ˋwʌndɚ]	納悶；想知道
schedule [ˋskɛdʒʊl]	時間表；課程表；（火車等的）時刻表
check [tʃɛk]	檢查，檢驗，核對
yacht [jɑt]	快艇；遊艇
out of town	出城，不在城裡
shame [ʃem]	憾事；倒霉的事
invite [ɪnˋvaɪt]	邀請；招待
invitation [ˌɪnvəˋteʃən]	(n.) 邀請
though [ðo] (	一般放在句尾）然而，還是
Cheers [tʃɪrz]	謝謝（英式英語，非正式的場合中使用）；（敬酒時）大家乾杯
Come over	順便來訪
housewarming	喬遷慶宴
attend [əˋtɛnd]	出席，參加
sick [sɪk]	病的，有病的
regret [rɪˋgrɛt]	(n.) 懊悔，悔恨；抱歉，遺憾
available [əˋveləb!]	有空的，可與之聯繫的
pleasure [ˋplɛʒɚ]	愉快，高興；樂事
hospitality [ˌhɑspɪˋtælətɪ]	好客；殷勤招待
both [boθ]	兩者（都）；兩個（都）；雙方（都）
wonderful [ˋwʌndɚfəl]	極好的；精彩的；驚人的；奇妙的；非同尋常的
the other day	幾天前(前幾天)

track 14

1.10 打電話

會話實例

A Hello, this is Charlotte from the customer service department. How may I help you?

哈囉，我是客服組的夏綠蒂，請問有什麼事？

B Hi, it's Kelly speaking. May I speak to Mindy, please?

嗨，我是凱莉，我想找明蒂。

A Hold on, please.

請稍等一下。

B Thank you.

謝謝。

A She's not in the office. Would you like to leave a message?

她不在辦公室，你需要留言嗎？

B Could you ask her to call me back?

你可以請她回電給我嗎？

A Certainly.

好的。

交際篇

B Thank you.
謝謝。

延伸例句

▶ I'd like to speak to Brian, please.
我想找布萊恩。

▶ May I ask who's calling, please?
請問哪裡找？

▶ Hold the line, please.
請稍等。

▶ Could you hold on, please?
你可以稍等一下嗎？

▶ Just a moment, please.
請稍等。

▶ One moment, please.
請稍等。

▶ Could you call back later?
你可以稍後再回撥嗎？

▶ Could you call back in a few minutes?
你可以幾分鐘後再回撥嗎？

▶ Can I leave a message?
我可以留言嗎？

▶ Would you like to leave a message?
你想要留言嗎？

▶ Can I take a message?
你要留言嗎？

▶ Pardon me?
不好意思？

▶ Could you repeat that, please?
你可以再重複一次嗎？

▶ I'm sorry. I didn't catch what you just said.
不好意思，我剛才沒有聽到你說的話。

▶ I'm afraid you've got the wrong number.
你恐怕打錯電話了。

▶ Sorry. I think you've dialed the wrong number.
抱歉，我想你打錯號碼了。

▶ Oh, I'm sorry. I have the wrong number.
噢，抱歉，我打錯了。

▶ I must have the wrong number.
我一定是打錯號碼了。

▶ I guess I have the wrong number.
我猜我打錯了。

▶ Thank you for calling.
謝謝你的來電。

相關單字、片語

customer services	客戶服務部
department [dɪ`pɑrtmənt]	部；司；局；處；科；部門
hold on	緊握；不掛電話
message [`mɛsɪdʒ]	信息；消息
moment [`momənt]	瞬間；片刻
one moment	一會兒，等一等，稍等
repeat [rɪ`pit]	重複；重做；重說
dial [`daɪəl]	撥（電話號碼）；打電話給

🎧 track 15

1.11

與朋友聯絡感情

會話實例

🅐 Hey, Vincent, how are you?

嘿，文森，你好嗎？

🅑 Hi, Carl, I'm good, thank you.

嗨，卡爾，我很好，謝謝。

🅐 Oh man, it's been a while.

天哪，好久不見。

🅑 Yea, how have you been?

對呀，你最近過得如何？

A I've been busy with work lately.
我最近工作很忙。

B Do you wanna go grab a drink tonight?
你今晚不想一起去喝一杯？

A Yea, sure. I'll see you around 18:30 at Long Bar?
好呀，六點半在龍酒吧見？

B Ok, see you then!
好的，到時見！

交際篇

延伸例句

▶ It's been a while.
好久不見。

▶ Long time no see.
好久不見。

▶ Are you free to catch up for coffee after class?
你下課後有空一起喝杯咖啡聊聊近況嗎？

▶ Do you wanna grab a bite after your meeting?
你會議結束後要不要一起吃點東西？

▶ Are you doing anything on Sunday? Maybe we could hang out?
你禮拜天要做什麼？或許我們可以出去玩？

▶ What are you doing tonight? Do you want to come over for dinner?

你今天晚上要做什麼？要不要來我家吃晚餐？

▶ Would you like to go watch a movie this weekend?

你這週末想不想一起去看電影？

▶ Do you want to go to the indoor climbing centre after work?

你下班後想不想去室內攀岩場？

▶ We're going jogging tonight. Do you want to join us?

我們今晚要去慢跑，你要不要一起去？

▶ Do you feel like seeing a gig on Friday night?

你這禮拜五晚上要不要一起去看表演？

▶ I'm thinking of checking out that new restaurant and I was wondering if you would like to come.

我在想要去那家新開的餐廳試試，不知你想不想一起去？

▶ Thanks for inviting me. What time should I be there?

謝謝你邀請我，我幾點到好呢？

▶ I'd like to join you, but I have an online meeting this afternoon.

我很想一起去，但我下午要開線上會議。

▶ I'd love to stay, but I have a lot of work to do.
　我很想繼續待，但我有很多工作要做。

▶ I'd love to hang out with you, but I have to study for my exam tomorrow.
　我很想跟你一起出去晃晃，但我要為明天的考試做準備。

▶ Thanks for asking, but I have other plans.
　謝謝你邀請我，但我有其他計畫了。

▶ Maybe another time.
　或許下次。

①交際篇

相關單字、片語

catch up	敘舊；聊聊
grab a bite	簡單吃點東西；吃點心
meeting [`mitɪŋ]	會議；集會
hang out	常去某處；居住；出去玩、消磨時間、到外面晃晃
indoor [`ɪnˌdor]	室內的
jog [dʒɑg]	慢跑
join [dʒɔɪn]	參加；同……一起
gig [gɪg]	（爵士樂、搖滾樂等）演奏，公演

1.12 加油打氣

會話實例

Ⓐ I'm so worried about the exams.
考試讓我好煩惱。

Ⓑ Why? You've put a lot of effort into studying.
為什麼？你花了這麼多精力讀書。

Ⓐ I'm just nervous. I failed the math exam last time.
我很緊張，我數學考試上次不及格。

Ⓑ Come on. You can do it.
加油，你可以的。

Ⓐ I probably just need to relax.
我大概只是需要放鬆。

Ⓑ Exactly. I have faith in you!
沒錯，我對你有信心！

Ⓐ Cheers.
謝拉。

Ⓑ Hang in there!
撐著點。

延伸例句

▶ Hang in there!
撐著點/ 不要洩氣/ 堅持下去！

▶ I'm with you.
我支持你。

▶ I'm rooting for you.
我支持你。

▶ I'm on your side.
我支持你。

▶ You've got this!
你沒問題的！

▶ I've got your back.
我挺你。

▶ You're almost there.
你已經快成功了。

▶ Keep your chin up.
不要氣餒。

▶ Go for it, you can do it!
去吧，你可以做到的！

▶ I have confidence in your ability.
我對你的能力有信心。

▶ Everything will work out.
事情會好轉的。

▶ Keep it up.
繼續努力。

▶ Stick to it.
堅持下去。

▶ Cheer up!
振作點！加油！

▶ Way to go!
做得好！

相關單字、片語

exam [ɪg`zæm]	examination的縮寫，(口語)考試
effort [`ɛfɚt]	努力，盡力
nervous [`nɜvəs]	神經質的；緊張不安的
fail [fel]	失敗；不及格
probably [`prɑbəblɪ]	大概，或許
relax [rɪ`læks]	放鬆；緩和
Exactly [ɪg`zæktlɪ]	確切地，精確地；完全地；恰好地
faith [feθ]	信念；信任
hang [hæŋ]	把……掛起；絞死
root for	支持，聲援

Stick [stɪk]	停留；堅持；固守
chin [tʃɪn]	下巴
confidence [`kɑnfədəns]	自信，信心，把握
ability [ə`bɪlətɪ]	能力

track 17

表達關心

1.13

會話實例

A What's on your mind? You look worried.
你在想什麼？你看起來很擔心。

B My husband's company laid off 3000 people yesterday. He is one of them.
我先生的公司昨天裁員三千人，他是其中之一。

A Oh, I'm sorry to hear that.
喔，我聽了真的很難過。

B It's ok, there's nothing we could do about it.
沒關係，我們也無能為力。

A How is he holding up?
他還好嗎？

交際篇

B He's okay. He wants to take a break, paint the house before looking for a new job.

他還好，他想要再找新工作之前先休息一陣子、幫家裡粉刷。

A If he needs any help with painting, just let me know.

如果他有需要幫忙粉刷，可以跟我說。

B Sure, thank you.

好的，謝謝。

延伸例句

▶ Are you ok?
你還好嗎？

▶ What's going on?
怎麼回事？

▶ What's bothering you?
有什麼事讓你心煩嗎？

▶ Why the long face?
為什麼一臉不開心？

▶ How are you holding up?
你還好嗎？

▶ Look on the bright side.
往好處想／樂觀一點。

相關單字、片語

mind [maɪnd]	(n.) 頭腦，智力；記憶力；注意力；主意；意見，想法
worried [ˋwɝɪd]	擔心的，發愁的
lay off	解僱；停止使用；停止騷擾
break [brek]	暫停；休息
bother [ˋbɑðɚ]	麻煩，費心
bright [braɪt]	明亮的；發亮的

 track 18

1.14
表達生氣

會話實例

Ⓐ Oh no, not again.
喔不，又來了。

Ⓑ What's going on?
怎麼了？

Ⓐ My neighbors' dog is barking again.
鄰居的狗又在叫了。

Ⓑ Wow…That's very loud.
哇，好大聲。

A Yea, I've had enough! It's really getting on my nerves.

對，我受夠了！真的很煩人！

B Did you try to talk to your neighbors?

你有試著跟鄰居溝通嗎？

A Yes, but they can't do anything about it.

有啊，但他們也無能為力。

B Too bad!

太糟糕了！

延伸例句

▶ I've had enough!
我受夠了！

▶ I'm fed up!
我受夠了！

▶ I'm sick of your rude remarks!
我受夠你無禮的評論了！

▶ I can't stand it anymore!
我再也受不了了！

▶ The weather drives me crazy!
這天氣真的要讓我瘋了！

▶ Stop nagging. You're getting on my nerves.
不要再嘮叨了，你讓我感到厭煩。

▶ It winds me up.
這讓我很生氣。

▶ It makes me angry.
這讓我很生氣。

▶ I'm annoyed at his bchavior.
他的行為讓我很惱怒。

▶ His speech irritated me a little.
他的言論讓我有些惱怒。

▶ Politicians piss me off.
政治家讓我感到很生氣。

▶ Tom blew up when he found out his girlfriend was cheating on him.
湯姆在發現發現女友出軌後勃然大怒。

▶ Whenever I spend too much time playing video games, it gets to my girlfriend.
每次我打電動打太久，女友就會生氣。

▶ Mind your own business.
管好你自己的事。

▶ Leave me alone!
讓我靜一靜/ 別煩我！

▶ How annoying!
真討厭！

▶ Get out of my face!
走開！別煩我！

相關單字、片語

bark [bɑrk]	狗，狐等）吠叫
enough [əˋnʌf]	足夠的，充足的
feed [fid]	餵（養）；飼（養）[（+on/with）]；進（料）；投入；供給；提供
sick [sɪk]	對……厭煩的
rude [rud]	粗野的，粗魯的，無禮的；粗糙的，簡陋的
remark [rɪˋmɑrk]	言辭；談論，評論
stand [stænd]	忍受，容忍
anymore [ˋɛnɪmor]	（不）再，再也（不）
weather [ˋwɛðə]	天氣
nag [næg]	不斷嘮叨；責罵不休
nerve [nɝv]	神經
wind sb. up	使生氣
behavior [bɪˋhevjə]	行為，舉止；態度
speech [spitʃ]	說話，言詞，言論
irritate [ˋɪrətet]	使惱怒；使煩躁；使過敏
Politician [ˏpɑləˋtɪʃən]	從事政治者，政治家；【貶】專搞黨派政治的人，政客
piss sb. off	使某人惱怒或厭煩
pissed off	生氣的；厭煩的；惱火的

blow up	發脾氣；勃然大怒
find out	找出；發現；查明
business [ˋbɪznɪs]	職業；日常工作；生意，交易

2

機場篇

2.1 登機櫃臺手續

會話實例

🅐 Hi, may I have your passport, please?
嗨，可以給我您的護照嗎？

🅑 Here you go.
這裡。

🅐 Where are you flying?
您要去哪裡？

🅑 New York.
紐約。

🅐 Do you have any power banks in your checked baggage?
您的托運行李裡有行動電源嗎？

🅑 No, it's in my carry-on luggage.
沒有，在隨身行李裡。

🅐 Ok, please put your suitcase up here. Here's your boarding pass and passport. Your seat number is 48A. You'll be boarding at gate A7, boarding starts at 15:30.

2 機場篇

好的，您可以將行李放上來這裡。這是您的登機證
及護照，您的座位是 48A，登機門是 A7，登機時間
為下午三點半。

B Thank you very much!
非常感謝！

A My pleasure.
不客氣。

延伸例句

▶ My destination is Paris.
我的目的地是巴黎。

▶ How much is it to upgrade to business class?
升等到商務艙要多少錢？

▶ Do you prefer window seats or aisle seats?
請問您要坐靠窗或走道？

▶ Do you have any lighters in your checked
baggage?
您的托運行李中有打火機嗎？

▶ If your hand luggage contains any knives or
scissors, they will be confiscated.
若是您的手提行李中有任何的刀子及剪刀，會被沒
收。

▶ Are you checking any baggage?
請問您有要托運的行李嗎？

▶ What's my allowance for checked baggage?
請問我的行李限額是多少？

▶ I'm afraid there'll be an excess baggage charge.
恐怕您要付超重行李費。

▶ How much do I have to pay for excess baggage?
請問我要付多少超重費？

▶ How long is the flight?
請問飛行時間是多久？

▶ Please mark this bag as "fragile".
請幫我標記此行李為「易碎」。

▶ Please place your luggage on the scales.
請把您的行李放上來秤重。

▶ Please attach this tag on your hand luggage.
請將這個標籤繫在您的手提行李上。

▶ Your flight departs from gate 35E and boarding starts at 10:20.
請由35E登機門上機，登機時間十點二十分。

▶ Please proceed to the gate before 17:30.
請在下午五點半前抵達登機門。

▶ This is the final boarding call for flight Ek 366 to Taipei.
這是Ek366班機前往台北的最後廣播。

②
機
場
篇

相關單字、片語

passport [ˋpæsˌport]	護照	
power bank	行動電源	
baggage [ˋbægɪdʒ]	行李[U]	
carry-on baggage	隨身攜帶的行李	
suitcase [ˋsutˌkes]	小型旅行箱	
boarding pass	登機證	
board [bord]	上（船，車，飛機等）	
gate [get]	大門；柵欄門；登機門	
destination [ˌdɛstəˋneʃən]	目的地，終點	
upgrade [ˋʌpˋgred]	使升級；提高；提升	
window [ˋwɪndo]	窗，窗戶	
aisle [aɪl]	通道，走道	
lighter [ˋlaɪtɚ]	打火機；點火器	
contain [kənˋten]	包含；容納；控制	
knife [naɪf]	刀，小刀；菜刀	
scissors [ˋsɪzɚz]	剪刀	
confiscate [ˋkɑnfɪsˌket]	沒收，將……充公	
allowance [əˋlaʊəns]	津貼，補貼；零用錢；分配額；允許額	
excess [ɪkˋsɛs]	過量的；額外的；附加的	
scale [skel]	天平，秤	
attach [əˋtætʃ]	裝上，貼上，繫上	
tag [tæg]	牌子，標籤，貨籤	
depart [dɪˋpart]	起程，出發；離開，離去	
proceed [prəˋsid]	行進	

登機找位子

會話實例

Ⓐ Excuse me, I can't find my seat.
不好意思，我找不到我的位置。

Ⓑ May I see your boarding pass?
可以給我看您的登機證嗎？

Ⓐ Here you are.
這邊。

Ⓑ Your seat is 26D, this way please.
您的座位是26D，這邊請。

Ⓐ Thank you very much. Where is the lavatory?
非常感謝您。請問廁所在哪裡？

Ⓑ It's over there.
在那邊。

Ⓐ Thank you. May I use it now?
謝謝，我現在可以使用嗎？

Ⓑ Yes, you can use it whenever the fasten seat belt sign is off.
可以，只要安全帶指示燈熄滅時都可以使用。

❷ 機場篇

延伸例句

▶ Welcome on board.
歡迎登機。

▶ Is it possible to swap seats?
請問可以換座位嗎？

▶ Can I move to the emergency exit row if no one is sitting there?
請問若是沒有人坐的話，我可以換到逃生門那排嗎？

▶ For an extra fee, you can stretch your legs in the extra legroom seats.
支付額外費用，您便可以在寬敞席伸展雙腳。

▶ How much does extra legroom cost?
寬敞席(加長伸腿空間座位)要多少錢？

▶ When the seat belt sign is illuminated, passengers should remain in their seats.
當安全帶指示燈亮起，乘客應該要留在座位上坐好。

▶ If you need anything, please press the call bell.
如果您需要任何服務，請按服務鈴。

▶ Can I move to the window seat?
我可以換去窗邊座位嗎？

▶ Can I change to the empty seat over there?
我可以換去那邊的空位嗎？

▶ Do you mind exchanging seats with me?
你介意跟我換位子嗎？

▶ I'm traveling with my friend, we'd like to sit next to each other.
我跟朋友一起旅行想坐在一起。

▶ Is it possible that we swap seats?
請問我們能換位子嗎？

▶ I'd much appreciate it if I could sit next to my wife.
我會非常感激，如果我能跟我的太太一起坐。

▶ Can you hang my jacket?
你可以幫我掛外套嗎？

▶ Is the flight on time?
飛機會准點起飛嗎？

2 機場篇

相關單字、片語

seat [sit]	座位
lavatory [ˋlævəˌtorɪ]	洗手間
whenever [hwɛnˋɛvə]	無論什麼時候；每當
fasten [ˋfæsn̩]	紮牢；繫緊；閂住；釘牢
seat belt [ˈsiːt belt]	安全帶
on board	上船，上飛機，上火車
possible [ˋpɑsəb!]	可能的
swap [swɑp]	交換；以……作交換

emergency [ɪ`mɝ·dʒənsɪ]	緊急情況
exit [`ɛksɪt]	出口，通道
row [raʊ]	（一）列，（一）排； （一排）座位
fee [fi]	費用
extra [`ɛkstrə]	額外的；外加的；另外收費的
stretch [strɛtʃ]	伸直；伸出；伸長；拉直； 拉緊；拉長；撐大
legroom [`lɛɡ͵rum]	（車輛，飛機，劇院等座位 的）放腳空間；踏腳處
illuminated [ɪ`lumə͵netɪd]	被照明的；發光的
passenger [`pæsndʒɚ]	乘客，旅客
remain [rɪ`men]	留下；逗留
travel [`træv!]	旅行
friend [frɛnd]	朋友
jacket [`dʒækɪt]	夾克，上衣
on time	準時

🎧 track 21

2.3 購買免稅商品

會話實例

A How may I help you?

您需要什麼嗎？

B Could I please have a gin and tonic?

我可以點一杯琴湯尼嗎？

A Yes, would you like some ice and lemon?

好的，您要加冰塊跟檸檬嗎？

B Oh yes, please. And can I see this watch in the magazine when you're ready? It's my son's birthday, I want to buy him a present.

喔好的，麻煩你。等你準備好時，我可以看雜誌上的這只手錶嗎？今天是我兒子生日，我想要買個禮物給他。

A Sure, I'll be right back.

好的，我馬上回來。

B Thank you very much.

非常感謝您。

A You're welcome. Do you mind resetting the call bell by pressing it again?

不客氣，您介意幫我再按一次以便重設服務鈴嗎？

B No problem!

沒問題！

延伸例句

▶ I'd like to buy this item.

我想要買這個品項。

▶ Can I open it?
我可以打開嗎？

▶ Do you have reading glasses?
你們有賣老花眼鏡嗎？

▶ Do you have toys for kids?
你們有賣小孩的玩具嗎？

▶ Sorry to let you know that we ran out of this product.
很抱歉讓您知道這個產品賣完了。

▶ Today we have a promotion, buy two perfumes, get 20% off.
今天我們有促銷活動，買兩瓶香水就打八折。

▶ Would you like to get two, the second one is 50% off.
您要買兩個嗎？第二件半價。

▶ How much is this one?
這個要多少錢？

▶ Which currencies can I pay in?
有哪些國家的貨幣可以用來付款？

▶ Can I pay in a different currency?
我可以用不同的貨幣付款嗎？

▶ Can I pay by credit card?
我可以刷卡嗎？

▶ You can pay with a credit card or in cash.
您可以用信用卡或現金付款。

▶ Do you take Japanese yen?
你們接受日幣嗎？

▶ We don't accept debit cards.
我們不接受金融卡。

▶ Please sign here.
請在這裡簽名。

▶ Here is your receipt.
這是您的收據。

▶ Thank you for shopping with us.
謝謝您的購買。

▶ Can I have a bag?
可以給我一個袋子嗎？

相關單字、片語

watch [wɑtʃ]	錶，手錶
magazine [ˌmægəˋzin]	雜誌，期刊
present [ˋprɛznt]	禮物
reset [riˋsɛt]	重置，清零重新設定，重新組合
press [prɛs]	按，壓，擠
again [əˋgɛn]	再，再一次

item [ˋaɪtəm]	項目；品目
reading glasses	老花鏡；放大鏡
toy [tɔɪ]	玩具，玩物
run out	用完，耗盡
product [ˋprɑdəkt]	產品，產物
promotion [prəˋmoʃən]	推銷運動
perfume [pɚˋfjum]	香水
different [ˋdɪfərənt]	不同的
currency [ˋkɝ-ənsɪ]	通貨，貨幣
credit card	信用卡
japanese [͵dʒæpəˋniz]	日本（人）的；日語的
yen [jɛn]	日圓（日本貨幣單位）
accept [əkˋsɛpt]	接受
debit card	借方卡；扣賬卡
sign [saɪn]	簽名
receipt [rɪˋsit]	收據

🎧 track 22

2.4

機上娛樂系統

會話實例

🅐 Excuse me. How long does it take before we land?

不好意思，距離我們降落還有多久時間？

B About 3 hours, you can also find the flight information on your screen.

大約三小時，您也可以從銀幕上看到飛行相關資訊。

A My screen is not working.

我的銀幕壞掉了。

B I'm really sorry about that. Please do not touch the screen for 10 minutes, we'll reset it for you.

我真的感到很抱歉，請您等待十分鐘，先不要觸碰銀幕，我們將會為您重新設定。

(After 10 minutes)

B Hello, is it working properly now?

哈囉，請問您的銀幕能正常運作了嗎？

A Yes, thank you. Are there movies in Mandarin?

可以了，謝謝。請問有中文電影嗎？

B Yes, Just tap on the entertainment system on the touch screen and choose "Movies," then choose "Mandarin Movies."

有的，只要從輕敲觸控銀幕點選娛樂系統，然後選擇「電影」，再選取「中文電影」。

A I got it, thanks.

我了解了，謝謝。

延伸例句

▶ How do you turn off the screen?
　請問要怎麼把銀幕關掉。

▶ Where do I plug the headphones?
　請問耳機插頭要插哪裡？

▶ How do I increase the volume?
　請問要如何把音量調大聲？

相關單字、片語

before [bɪ`for]	在……以前
land [lænd]	登陸；降落
information [ˌɪnfə`meʃən]	報告；消息；資訊
screen [skrin]	螢幕；銀幕
properly [`prɑpəlɪ]	恰當地；正確地
movie [`muvɪ]	電影，影片
Mandarin [`mændərɪn]	華語
tap [tæp]	輕拍，輕叩，輕敲；（手指或觸摸筆）點擊（螢幕）
entertainment [ˌɛntə`tenmənt]	娛樂
touch [tʌtʃ]	接觸，碰到；觸摸
turn off	關掉 頭戴式耳機
plug [plʌg]	接通電源；連接
headphones [`hɛdˌfonz]	耳機
wake up	醒來；弄醒

increase [ɪnˋkris]	增大;增加;增強
volume [ˋvɑljəm]	音量

2.5 機上用餐

會話實例

🅐 We are serving beef ragout and chicken curry today, which one would you like to have?

我們今天有牛肉燉菜和雞肉咖哩,請問您想吃哪一個?

🅑 What does it come with beef ragout?

牛肉燉菜裡面有什麼?

🅐 Beef ragout is served with potato wedges, chicken curry is with rice.

牛肉燉菜有馬鈴薯角,雞肉咖哩是跟飯一起。

🅑 I'll take chicken curry.

請給我雞肉咖哩。

🅐 Here you go. Would you like some drinks?

給您,您想要喝點什麼嗎?

B Can I have a diet coke?

可以給我健怡可樂嗎？

A Certainly. Enjoy your meal.

當然，請享用。

B Thank you very much.

非常謝謝你。

延伸例句

▷ Please don't wake me up for the meal service.

請不要在餐點服務時把我叫醒。

▷ When will the next service start?

下個餐點服務何時開始？

▷ I'm hungry, is it ok if I take a banana?

我肚子很餓，我可以拿一根香蕉嗎？

▷ Would you like to have breakfast?

您想用早餐嗎？

▷ We are serving omelette and scrambled eggs.

我們有歐姆蛋跟炒蛋。

▷ Would you care for a drink?

您想喝點什麼嗎？

▷ What kind of wines do you serve today?

你們今天供應哪些酒？

▶ What drinks do you offer?
你們提供什麼飲料？

▶ We have red wine, white wine, beers, cocktails, juices and soft drinks.
我們提供紅酒、白酒、啤酒、調酒、果汁和氣泡飲料。

▶ Can I have some orange juice?
可以給我柳橙汁嗎？

▶ Can I please have a glass of water?
可以給我一杯水嗎？

▶ Would you care for some tea or coffee?
您要茶或咖啡嗎？

▶ Coffee with two milk and four sugar.
請給我咖啡和兩個奶球跟四包糖。

▶ Here is your special meal.
這是您的特別餐。

▶ Did you order a Non-Lactose meal?
您有點無乳糖餐嗎？

▶ Can I have the baby meal for my baby, please?
可以給我嬰兒餐嗎？

▶ I've ordered a child meal for my kid.
我訂了兒童餐給我的小孩。

▶ Do you have infant formula?
　請問有嬰兒奶粉嗎？

▶ Do you have a vegetarian option?
　請問有素食選擇嗎？

▶ I'm vegan, but I forgot to order a vegan meal.
　我吃全素，但是我忘記訂素食餐了。

▶ I'll see what I can do.
　我會看看能做些什麼。

▶ If we have extra vegan meals, I'll bring it to you.
　如果我們有額外的素食餐，我會拿給你。

▶ Can you heat up the milk for me?
　請問你可以幫我加熱牛奶嗎？

相關單字、片語

serve [sɝv]	服務；招待，侍候；上酒，端菜
ragout [ræˋgu]	【法】蔬菜燉肉；五香雜燴
certainly [ˋsɝtənlɪ]	（用於回答）當然；可以；沒問題
meal [mil]	膳食；一餐
diet [ˋdaɪət]	n. 飲食，食物；（適合某種疾病的）特種飲食 vi. 進規定的飲食；忌食；節食
service [ˋsɝvɪs]	服務；效勞；幫助
hungry [ˋhʌŋgrɪ]	飢餓的；顯出飢餓樣子的

breakfast [`brɛkfəst]	早餐
omelette [`ɑmlɪt]	煎蛋餅，煎蛋捲
scramble [`skræmb!]	炒（蛋）
care for	喜歡
milk [mɪlk]	乳；牛奶
cocktail `kɑk,tel]	雞尾酒；（西餐的）開胃品
soft drink	汽水
lactose [`læktos]	乳糖
infant [`ɪnfənt]	嬰兒
formula [`fɔrmjələ]	配製成的嬰兒奶粉或奶水
vegetarian [,vɛdʒə`tɛrɪən] adj. 素食主義者的； 吃素的 n.素食者	
option [`ɑpʃən]	選擇
order [`ɔrdə]	定購；點菜
vegan [`vɛgən]	嚴格素食主義者
forget [fə`gɛt]	忘記
heat up	把……加熱

 🎧 track 24

2.6 慶祝紀念日

會話實例

Ⓐ Hi, can we have 2 bottles of champagne?
嗨，可以給我們兩瓶香檳嗎？

B Yes, sure. Would you like to pay by credit card or by cash?

好的,您要用信用卡還是現金付款?

A I'll pay with a credit card.

用信用卡付。

B Are you celebrating a special occasion?

您們要慶祝什麼特別的活動嗎?

A Yes, today is our wedding anniversary.

是的,今天是我們的結婚週年紀念日。

B That's amazing! If I may ask, how long have you been married?

太棒了!您介意我知道您們結婚多久了嗎?

A 25 years.

二十五年。

B Wow! Happy 25th anniversary!

哇!二十五週年快樂!

延伸例句

▶ Can I take a polaroid picture for you?
我可以幫您拍張立可拍嗎?

▶ Happy Birthday to you!
祝你生日快樂!

▶ Your friend ordered a cake for you.
你的朋友訂了一個蛋糕給你。

▶ We prepared a cake and some flowers for your wife.

我們準備了蛋糕和花要給你太太。

相關單字、片語

bottle [`bɑt!]	瓶子
champagne [ʃæm`pen]	香檳酒；香檳酒色
celebrate [`sɛləˌbret]	慶祝，過節；舉行
special [`spɛʃəl]	特別的，特殊的
occasion [ə`keʒən]	場合，時刻；重大活動，盛典
wedding [`wɛdɪŋ]	結婚典禮；結婚紀念日
anniversary [ˌænə`vɝ·sərɪ]	週年紀念；週年紀念日；結婚週年
amazing [ə`mezɪŋ]	驚人的，令人吃驚的
married [`mærɪd]	已婚的，有配偶的；婚姻的；夫婦的
polaroid [`poləˌrɔɪd	（商標名）拍立得一次成像照相機（或照片）
prepare [prɪ`pɛr]	準備
flower [`flauə·]	花

track 25

2.7 填寫入境表

會話實例

🅐 Hello, madame, is your final destination Singapore or Melbourne?

哈囉，女士，您的最終目的地是新加坡還是墨爾本？

🅑 Singapore.

新加坡。

🅐 Here is a health declaration form and a landing card for you.

這是您的健康聲明表及入境卡。

🅐 What are these for?

這些是要做什麼用的？

🅑 The Customs in Singapore require you to fill out these forms.

新加坡海關要求您填寫這些表格。

🅑 Can I borrow a pen?

可以跟你借支筆嗎？

🅐 Sure, I'll bring you one right away.

好的，我馬上拿給您。

B Thank you.

謝謝。

延伸例句

▶ What is the flight number?
請問航班號碼是什麼？

▶ What's the date today?
今天是幾月幾號？

▶ Can I have another form?
可以再給我一張表格嗎？

相關單字、片語

final [ˈfaɪnl]	最後的；最終的
health [hɛlθ]	健康
declaration [ˌdɛkləˈreʃən]	宣布，宣告；宣言，聲明
form [fɔrm]	表格
card [kɑrd]	卡片
custom [ˈkʌstəm]	（常大寫）海關
require [rɪˈkwaɪr]	要求，命令
fill out	填寫（表格、申請書等）
borrow [ˈbɑro]	借，借入
bring [brɪŋ]	帶來，拿來
right away	立刻，馬上
number [ˈnʌmbɚ]	數，數字
date [det]	日期，日子
another [əˈnʌðɚ]	又一，再一；另一；另外的

2.8 要東西

會話實例

Ⓐ Hi, how can I help you?

嗨,需要幫忙嗎?

Ⓑ Hi, I was wondering if I could borrow a pen?

嗨,我可以跟你借支筆嗎?

Ⓐ Sure, here you go. Do you need anything else? We have eye shades, socks, and earplugs.

當然,來,給你。你需要其他東西嗎?我們有眼罩、襪子跟耳塞。

Ⓑ Excellent! Can I have them all?

太棒了!我可以都要嗎?

Ⓐ Sure. One moment, please. Here you go.

當然,請稍等我一下。給你。

Ⓑ Thank you very much! I'll return the pen once I'm done.

太感謝了!筆用完之後我會拿來還你。

A Don't worry, you can keep it. Have a nice flight!

別擔心,你可以留著。飛行愉快!

B Thank you.

謝謝。

延伸例句

▶ Do you happen to have a blue pen?
你剛好有藍筆嗎?

▶ Do you provide toothpicks?
你們有提供牙籤嗎?

▶ Can I have a toothbrush, please?
可以給我一支牙刷嗎?

▶ Is it possible to have an extra blanket?
可以再多給我一個毛毯嗎?

▶ Can I have two more pillows?
可以多給我兩個枕頭嗎?

▶ Do you have a band-aid?
你有OK繃嗎?

▶ I was wondering if you have pain-killers.
你們有止痛藥嗎?

▶ Can I have a baby bottle?
可以給我一個奶瓶嗎?

②機場篇

▶ Could you give me some ice? I sprained my ankle.

可以麻煩你給我一些冰塊嗎？我扭到腳了。

相關單字、片語

need [nid]	需要
shade [ʃed]	遮光物
sock [sɑk]	短襪
earplug [ˋɪrˏplʌg]	耳塞
excellent [ˋɛksḷənt]	出色的；傑出的；優等的
moment [ˋmomənt]	瞬間；片刻
return [rɪˋtɝn]	還，歸還
once [wʌns]	一旦，一經……便
done [dʌn]	完成了的，做完的
worry [ˋwɝɪ]	憂慮，擔心
keep [kip]	擁有；保管
blue [blu]	藍色的
provide [prəˋvaɪd]	提供
happen to	碰巧
toothpick [ˋtuθˏpɪk]	牙籤
toothbrush [ˋtuθˏbrʌʃ]	牙刷
blanket [ˋblæŋkɪt]	毛毯，毯子
pillow [ˋpɪlo]	枕頭
band-aid [ˋbændˏed]	邦迪創可貼（商標名，一種護創膠布，台灣常稱 OK繃）

pain-killer [penˌkɪlə]	【口】鎮痛劑、止痛藥
bottle [`bɑt!]	瓶子
sprain [spren]	扭傷
ankle [`æŋk!]	踝，足踝

🎧 track 27

2.9 緊急醫療狀況

會話實例

🅐 Hello, can you please have a look at my son?

哈囉，可以請你看看我的兒子嗎？

🅑 Yes, what happened?

好的，怎麼了？

🅐 I think he's choking.

我想他噎到了。

🅑 Continue coughing! (talking to the boy)

（對男孩說）繼續咳嗽！

🅐 He's not breathing!

他沒呼吸了！

B Can you hear me? (talking to the boy) Get the senior and AED! I'm starting CPR. (Talking to other crew)

（對男孩說）你聽得到嗎？（對其他組員說）幫我找主管並且拿體外電擊器來！我要開始進行心肺復甦術。

A What can I do to help?

我可以幫什麼忙嗎？

B Help me put him on the floor.

幫我把他移到地上。

延伸例句

▶ I feel unwell.

我不舒服。

▶ I'm feeling nauseous.

我感到想吐。

▶ I had diarrhea.

我拉肚子。

▶ I vomited three times.

我吐了三次。

▶ I have a severe headache.

我頭痛很嚴重。

▶ I feel very cold and thirsty.

我感到很冷又很渴。

▶ He has a slight fever.
他輕度發燒。

▶ He has a severe allergic reaction.
他有嚴重過敏反應。

▶ Do you have a thermometer?
你有溫度計嗎？

▶ The thermometer reads 39 degrees celsius.
溫度計上的讀數是攝氏三十九度。

▶ Can I have a glass of warm water?
可以給我一杯溫水嗎？

▶ How do you feel?
你感覺如何？

▶ Do you feel better?
你有感到好點嗎？

▶ When is the last time you eat?
你上次吃東西是什麼時候？

▶ What are the symptoms?
你有哪些症狀？

▶ Have you ever encountered this situation before?
你以前有遇過相同情況嗎？

▶ Do you have your own medication?
你有自己的藥品嗎？

❷ 機場篇

▶ Have you had any major illnesses or surgeries?
你曾經有過重大疾病或手術嗎？

▶ Do you have any chronic disease?
您有任何慢性病嗎？

▶ Is there anything you are allergic to?
您有對任何東西過敏嗎？

▶ Do you have any drug and food allergies?
您有任何藥物或食物過敏嗎？

▶ Can you please store my medication in the refrigerator for me?
可以請你幫我把藥物放在冰箱嗎？

▶ Sure, may I have your boarding pass?
當然，可以給我您的登機證嗎？

▶ I have diabetes.
我有糖尿病。

▶ I have asthma.
我有氣喘。

▶ He fainted away at the sight of blood.
他一看到血就昏倒了。

▶ I feel as if I'm going to faint.
我感到好像要暈倒似的。

相關單字、片語

look [lʊk]	看
happen [ˋhæpən]	發生
choke [tʃok]	窒息;嗆住;説不出話來
continue [kənˋtɪnjʊ]	繼續,持續
cough [kɔf]	咳嗽
breath [brɛθ]	呼吸,氣息
hear [hɪr]	聽見;聽
senior [ˋsinjɚ]	較年長者;前輩;上司;學長;資深人士
AED (automated external defibrillator) 自動體外心臟去顫器或稱自動體外電擊器	
start [stɑrt]	出發,起程;開始,著手
CPR (cardiopulmonary resuscitation) 心肺復甦術	
floor [flor]	地板,地面
unwell [ʌnˋwɛl]	不舒服的,有病的
nauseous [ˋnɔʃɪəs]	想嘔吐的
diarrhea [ˌdaɪəˋriə]	腹瀉
vomit [ˋvɑmɪt]	嘔吐
severe [səˋvɪr]	嚴重的;劇烈的
headache [ˋhɛdˌek]	頭痛
cold [kold]	冷的,寒冷的
thirsty [ˋθɝstɪ]	口乾的,渴的
fever [ˋfivɚ]	發燒
allergic [əˋlɝdʒɪk]	過敏的
reaction [rɪˋækʃən]	反應,感應

better [ˈbɛtə]	較佳的；更好的
thermometer [θəˈmɑmətə]	溫度計
degree [dɪˈgri]	度，度數
celsius [ˈsɛlsɪəs]	百分度的；攝氏的
warm [wɔrm]	溫暖的，暖和的
symptom [ˈsɪmptəm]	症狀，徵候
encounter [ɪnˈkaʊntə]	遭遇；遇到；意外地遇見
situation [ˌsɪtʃʊˈeʃən]	處境，境遇；形勢； 情況；局面
medication [ˌmɛdɪˈkeʃən]	藥物治療；藥物
major [ˈmedʒə]	較大的；較多的；較大範 圍的；主要的，重要的
illnesses [ˈɪlnɪs]	患病（狀態）；身體 不適；（某種）疾病
surgery [ˈsɝdʒərɪ]	外科，外科醫學； （外科）手術
chronic [ˈkrɑnɪk]	（病）慢性的
disease [dɪˈziz]	病，疾病
allergy [ˈælədʒɪ]	過敏症
store [stor]	貯存
refrigerator [rɪˈfrɪdʒəˌretə]	冰箱
diabetes [ˌdaɪəˈbitiz]	糖尿病
asthma [ˈæzmə]	氣喘
faint [fent]	昏厥，暈倒
at the sight of	一看見(就…)

突發狀況

會話實例

Ⓐ Ladies and gentlemen, we're passing through an area of rough air. Please return to your seat and fasten your seat belt.

各位女士及先生，我們正經過一個不穩定氣流的區域，請回到您的座位並繫好安全帶。

Ⓑ Can I go to the toilet quickly?

我可以很快地去一下廁所嗎？

Ⓐ I'm sorry, please use it while the seat belt sign is off.

我很抱歉，請在安全帶指示燈熄滅後使用。

Ⓑ I really need to go now.

我現在真地需要去。

Ⓐ Ok, you can use it, but it's at your own risk. Please be careful. It's quite bumpy.

好吧，您可以使用，但若有意外後果您要自行負責。請小心，現在很晃。

Ⓑ Thank you!

謝謝！

❷
機
場
篇

延伸例句

▶ We are experiencing some moderate turbulence.
我們正經歷一些中度亂流。

▶ Please refrain from using the toilet.
請勿使用廁所。

▶ We experienced a little turbulence. It freaked me out!
我們經歷了一點亂流。我嚇慘了！

▶ I feel dizzy because of turbulence.
因為亂流，我感到頭暈。

▶ I saw smoke coming from that lavatory.
我看到有煙從那間廁所飄出來。

▶ There's smoke coming from the hatrack.
有煙從機上頭頂置物箱飄出來。

▶ In the event of a sudden loss of cabin pressure, an oxygen mask will automatically appear in front of you.
萬一有突發的客艙失壓狀況，氧氣面罩會自動出現在您面前。

▶ To start the flow of oxygen, pull the mask towards you. Place it firmly over your nose and mouth.
請將面罩向您的方向拉以啟動氧氣流量。將面罩緊緊蓋住您的口鼻。

▶ If you are travelling with a child or someone who requires assistance, secure your mask first, and then assist the other person.

若是您與需要協助的兒童或親友同行，請先戴好您的氧氣面罩，再協助他人。

▶ In the unlikely event of an emergency landing and evacuation, leave your carry-on items behind.

若發生機率極低的緊急降落及緊急逃生，將您的隨身行李留在座位上。

▶ Please stay calm and follow the instructions from the cabin crew.

請保持冷靜並聽從空服員指示。

相關單字、片語

lady [ˋledɪ]	女士，夫人，小姐	
gentleman [ˋdʒɛnt!mən]	紳士；有教養的男子；先生，男士	
pass [pæs]	通過；經過	
through [θru]	穿過；通過	
area [ˋɛrɪə]	地區，區域	
rough [rʌf]	暴風雨的；狂暴的；劇烈的	
air [ɛr]	空氣；大氣	
return [rɪˋtɝn]	回，返回	

quickly [`kwɪklɪ]	快，迅速地；立即，馬上
while [hwaɪl]	當……的時候
really [`rɪəlɪ]	真地，確實
at your own risk	自擔風險(同意不要求賠償損失、損害等)
careful [`kɛrfəl]	仔細的；小心的
quite [kwaɪt]	完全，徹底；相當，頗
bumpy [`bʌmpɪ]	崎嶇不平的，坑坑窪窪的；顛簸的
experience [ɪk`spɪrɪəns]	經驗，體驗；經歷，閱歷
moderate [`mɑdərɪt]	中等的，適度的
turbulence [`tɝbjələns]	(海洋、天氣等的)狂暴；動亂，騷亂；亂流；湍流；(氣體等的)紊流
refrain [rɪ`fren]	忍住；抑制，節制；戒除
freak out	使某人感到極度的欣喜或不安；發飆
dizzy [`dɪzɪ]	頭暈目眩的；使人頭暈的；極高的；快速旋轉的
smoke [smok]	煙；煙狀物；煙霧
come [kʌm]	來；來到；發生；降臨；出現；(從……)產生
hatrack [`hæt͵ræk]	帽架
In the event of	假如發生了…事
sudden [`sʌdn]	突然的；意外的；迅速的，快的
loss [lɔs]	喪失；遺失

cabin [ˋkæbɪn]	客艙
pressure [ˋprɛʃɚ]	壓力
oxygen [ˋɑksədʒən]	氧；氧氣
mask [mæsk]	假面具；偽裝；遮蔽物； 防護面具；口罩
automatically [ˏɔtəˋmætɪk!ɪ]	自動地；無意識地， 不自覺地，機械地
appear [əˋpɪə(r)]	出現；顯露；似乎，看來好像
in front of	在某人/某物前面
flow [flo]	流；流動；流速
towards [təˋwɔrdz]	向，朝；面對；將近；大約
firmly [ˋfɚmlɪ]	堅固地；穩固地；堅定地； 堅決地
over [ˋovɚ]	在……之上，在正上方； （覆蓋）在……上面
child [tʃaɪld]	小孩，兒童
someone [ˋsʌm͵wʌn]	某人，有人
assistance [əˋsɪstəns]	援助，幫助
secure [sɪˋkjʊr]	把……弄牢；關緊；使安全； 掩護；保衛
assist [əˋsɪst]	幫助，協助
calm [kɑm]	鎮靜的，沉著的
follow [ˋfɑlo]	跟隨；接在……之後；聽從； 採用
instruction [ɪnˋstrʌkʃən]	命令，指示
cabin crew	（客機）航班空服員

heavy [ˋhɛvɪ]	重的，沉的；沉重有力的；劇烈的；熱烈的
unlikely [ʌnˋlaɪklɪ]	不太可能的；靠不住的；不可能發生的
emergency [ɪˋmɝdʒənsɪ]	緊急情況
evacuation [ɪˏvækjʊˋeʃən]	撤空；撤離
leave [liv]	離開（某處）；留給；留下
item [ˋaɪtəm]	項目；品目
behind [bɪˋhaɪnd]	在背後；向背後；（留）在原處；（遺留）在後

🎧 track 29

2.11

通關申報

會話實例

A May I have your passport?

可以給我您的護照嗎？

B Here you go.

給您。

A What's the purpose of your visit?

請問您來訪的目的。

B I'm visiting family.

我來拜訪家人。

A How long is your stay?

您會停留多久？

B 3 weeks.

三禮拜。

A Please look al the camera.

請看鏡頭。

B Sure.

好的。

延伸例句

▶ Where will you be staying?

您會住在哪裡？

▶ What is your final destination?

您的旅行最終目的地是哪裡？

▶ I was just here to transit.

我只是轉機。

▶ I'm here for vacation.

我來這邊度假。

▶ I'm here for business.

我來出差。

▶ Where is your last stop?

您的最終站是哪裡？

2
機場篇

▶ How long will you be staying in the U.S.?
您會在美國待多久時間？

▶ We're going to stay in France for 7 days.
我們將會在法國住七天。

▶ Do you have a return ticket?
您有回程的機票嗎？

▶ Do you have a return ticket to Hongkong?
妳有回香港的返程機票嗎？

▶ I have an open ticket.
我有一張沒有固定期限的機票。

▶ What's the address of the hotel you stay at?
你入住的飯店地址為？

▶ How much currency are you carrying with you?
您身上攜帶多少幣值？

▶ Do you bring any cash with you?
您身上有攜帶任何現金？

▶ Have you been here before?
你有來過本國嗎？

▶ Who packed your bags?
是誰打包您的行李的？

▶ Did you leave the bags alone at any time?
您有在任何時候讓您的行李落單嗎？

▶ Did you leave your cabin bag unattended at any time?
您有在任何時候讓您的行李箱呈現無人看管的情況嗎?

▶ Please place your finger on the digital fingerprint reader.
請將手指放在數位指紋閱讀機上。

▶ Please queue here.
請在這裡排隊。

▶ Can you please open your bag?
可以請您打開您的行李嗎?

▶ Do you have anything to declare?
您有東西需要申報嗎?

▶ Please fill in this customs baggage declaration form.
請填這份海關行李申報單。

▶ I have unaccompanied baggage to declare.
我有非隨行行李要申報。

▶ I have nothing to declare.
我沒有任何東西要申報。

▶ Do you have any liquor or cigarettes?
你有攜帶含酒精飲料或香菸嗎?

▶ These objects require to be declared.
這些物品必須申報。

相關單字、片語

單字	中文
purpose [ˋpɝpəs]	目的，意圖
visit [ˋvɪzɪt]	參觀；拜訪；探望
camera [ˋkæmərə]	照相機；電影攝影機
transit [ˋtrænsɪt]	中轉
vacation [veˋkeʃən]	休假；假期；休庭期；休假日
stop [stɑp]	停止；中止；終止；停車；停車站
currency [ˋkɝənsɪ]	通貨，貨幣
ticket [ˋtɪkɪt]	票，券；車票；入場券
carry [ˋkærɪ]	攜帶，佩帶
pack [pæk]	裝（箱）；給（某人）將（某物）裝入行李
alone [əˋlon]	單獨地；獨自地
at any time	在任何時候，隨時
unattended [ˏʌnəˋtɛndɪd]	無侍從的；無伴的；沒人照顧的；未被注意的
finger [ˋfɪŋgɚ]	手指；大拇指以外的手指
digital [ˋdɪdʒɪtl̩]	數位的；數字的
fingerprint [ˋfɪŋgɚ͵prɪnt]	指紋，指印
reader [ˋridɚ]	閱讀機
queue [kju]	排隊；排隊等候

declare [dɪˋklɛr]	申報（納稅品等）
unaccompanied [ˏʌnəˋkʌmpənɪd]	
	無伴侶的；無伴隨的
nothing [ˋnʌθɪŋ]	無事；無物；沒什麼
liquor [ˋlɪkɚ]	酒；含酒精飲料

🎧 track 30

2.12 領行李

會話實例

Ⓐ Where do we go now?
我們現在要去哪裡？

Ⓑ Baggage claim area.
提領行李處。

Ⓐ Where can we find our baggage?
我們要如何找到我們的行李？

Ⓑ Let's look for a baggage carousel board. It lists which carousel will have our flight's bags.
我們找找看行李傳送帶公告牌，上面會列出我們班機的行李傳送帶。

Ⓐ Over there!
在那邊！

Ⓑ It's number 7. Let's go.
是七號，我們走吧。

Ⓐ Shall we get a trolley?
我們要拿個推車嗎？

Ⓑ Good idea!
好主意！

延伸例句

▶ My bag is missing.
我的行李不見了。

▶ My bag is broken.
我的行李壞掉了。

▶ The wheel of my suitcase is missing.
行李箱上的輪子掉了。

▶ Our checked luggage is delayed.
我們的托運行李延遲抵達。

▶ Can I ask for compensation?
我可以要求賠償嗎？

▶ Let's go to the baggage services desk.
我們去行李服務櫃檯。

▶ You can use your reference number to check the status of your baggage.
您可以用這個編號來查詢行李狀況。

▶ Hurry up! We have to go catch the next flight.
快點！我們要去趕下一班飛機。

相關單字、片語

claim [klem]	要求,認領
look for	尋找；期待
baggage carousel 行李傳送帶	
carousel [ˌkærʊˋzɛl]	旋轉木馬
board [bord]	牌子；布告牌
list [lɪst]	把……編列成表，把……編入目錄；列舉
shall [ʃæl]	（用在問句中表示徵求對方意見，主要用於第一，第三人稱）……好嗎？要不要……？
trolley [ˋtrɑlɪ]	小車；臺車；手推車；手推餐車
idea [aɪˋdiə]	主意；打算
missing [ˋmɪsɪŋ]	缺掉的；失蹤的，行蹤不明的；找不到的
broken [ˋbrokən]	破碎的；損壞的；被破壞的；遭違背的
wheel [hwil]	輪子，車輪
delay [dɪˋle]	延緩；使延期；耽擱；延誤
compensation [ˌkɑmpənˋseʃən] 賠償金；補償金	
reference [ˋrɛfərəns]	參考，參照；參考文獻；出處；查詢；了解

機場篇

status [`stetəs]	情形，狀況，狀態
hurry [`hɝɪ]	使趕緊；催促；急派
hurry up	快一點

🎧 track 31

2.13 兌換外幣

會話實例

A Hello. I'd like to exchange US dollars for Taiwanese dollars, what's the exchange rate, please?

哈囉，我想要用美金換台幣。請問現在的匯率是多少？

B The exchange rate is 29.6 New Taiwan dollars for 1 US dollar.

1美元換29.5新台幣。

A Ok, I'd like to change 500 US Dollars.

好的，我想換500美元。

B Sure. That'll be 14,800 NTD.

好的，這樣是台幣1萬4千8百。

A Do you charge any fee?

你們有收手續費嗎？

B No. Please sign here.
沒有，請在這裡簽名。

A Sure.
好的。

B Here's your cash.
這是您的現金。

延伸例句

▶ How much would you like to change?
您想換多少錢？

▶ I want to change 1,000 US dollars.
我想換一千美元。

▶ I'd like to exchange Swiss francs to Taiwanese Dollars.
我想把瑞士法郎換成新台幣。

▶ Hi, I'd like to exchange 500 Australian dollars to US dollars.
嗨，我想要五百塊澳幣換成美金。

▶ I would like to change Taiwanese dollars into Japanese yen.
我想要用台幣換日幣。

▶ What's the exchange rate for euros?
歐元的匯率是多少？

②
機場篇

▶ Do you charge an extra fee?
你們有收額外費用嗎？

▶ We offer commission-free exchange.
我們提供免收費的換匯服務。

▶ Could I cash my traveler's check here?
我可以在這兌換我的旅行支票嗎？

▶ How much do you charge for the commision?
你們的費用是多少？

▶ Would you like that in large or small bills?
你想要大鈔還是小鈔？

▶ How do you want that? Big denomination or small bills?
您想要什麼樣的面額？大鈔還是小鈔？

▶ In fifties, please.
我想要五十元的鈔票，麻煩您。

相關單字、片語

exchange [ɪks`tʃendʒ]	交換；調換；兌換
dollar [`dɑləˈ]	（美，加等國）元；一元紙幣；一元硬幣
exchange rate	外匯率
rate [ret]	比例，率；比率
change [tʃendʒ]	兌換（錢）

charge [tʃɑrdʒ]	索價；收費
offer [ˋɔfɚ]	給予，提供；拿出，出示
commission [kəˋmɪʃən]	佣金
traveler's check	旅行支票
traveler [ˋtrævlɚ]	旅行者，旅客；遊客
check [tʃɛk]	支票
large [lɑrdʒ]	大的，寬大的；大規模的；多的，多量的，多數的
small [smɔl]	小的；小型的；少的，少量的；幾乎沒有的
bill [bɪl]	鈔票
denomination [dɪˌnɑməˋneʃən]	
（貨幣等的）面額；（度量衡等的）單位	

🎧 track 32

2.14 機場交通

會話實例

A How may I help you?
需要幫忙嗎？

B Where is the bus station, please?
請問公車站在哪裡？

A Go straight and turn right when you see a convenience store.

直走,看到一家便利商店後右轉。

B Where can I buy a ticket?

哪裡可以買票?

A There's a counter next to the bus station. You can purchase a ticket there. You can also pay on the bus.

公車站旁邊有一個櫃檯,你可以在那裡買票,也可以上公車後付款。

B Will I get change from the driver?

司機會找零嗎?

A Yes, they can give you change.

會的,他們可以找錢給你。

B Thank you!

謝謝!

延伸例句

▶ We have to take the tram to the arrival terminal.
我們要搭電車去入境航廈。

▶ This tram connects different terminals.
這電車連接不同航廈。

▶ I booked a ride from the airport to the city center.
我訂了一趟由機場到市中心的旅程。

▶ I booked an airport transfer to my hotel.
我訂了從機場到我飯店的接送服務。

▶ Is there a free shuttle to the hotel?
有到飯店的免費接駁車嗎？

▶ Where is the taxi stand?
計程車車站在哪裡？

▶ Where can I purchase a ticket?
我可以去哪裡買票？

▶ I'd like to have a return ticket to Bastille station.
我想要買一張去巴士底站的來回票。

▶ How long is the ride to Eiffel tower?
去艾非爾鐵塔的路程要多久？

相關單字、片語

station [`steʃən]	車站[C]；（各種機構的）站，所，局，署
straight [stret]	直，挺直地；直接地，一直地
convenience [kən`vinjəns]	方便；合宜；便利設施；方便的用具
store [stor]	店舖，店
counter [`kaʊntə]	櫃臺；櫃臺式長桌
purchase [`pɝtʃəs]	買，購買；贏得，獲得，努力取
driver [`draɪvə]	司機，駕駛員

②
機
場
篇

tram [træm]	有軌電車；電車軌道
arrival [əˋraɪv!]	到達；到來；達到
terminal [ˋtɝmən!]	末端；終點；極限；（火車，巴士等的）終點站；航空站；碼頭
connect [kəˋnɛkt]	連接，連結；（交通工具）銜接，聯運
book [bʊk]	預訂；預僱；預約
ride [raɪd]	騎；乘坐；搭乘；騎馬（或乘車）旅行，兜風
airport [ˋɛrˏport]	機場；航空站
city center	（城鎮的）商業區；中心區
center [ˋsɛntɚ]	中心；中央，中心點；中心區；人口集中地區；中心站
transfer [trænsˋfɝ]	調動；轉移；轉會；轉接
hotel [hoˋtɛl]	旅館；飯店
taxi stand	計程車車站
stand [stænd]	停車處，候車站
return ticket	來回票
free [fri]	免費的
shuttle [ˋʃʌt!]	往返兩地間的運輸工具；往返兩地間的運輸服務

交通工具篇

3

3.1 租車

會話實例

A I'd like to rent a car.
我想要租一臺車。

B What kind of car would you like to rent?
你想租什麼樣的車？

A What are my options?
我有什麼選擇？

B We have regular sedans, SUVs and compact cars.
我們有一般轎車、休旅車和小型車。

A I'll take an SUV. How much would it cost per day?
我要租休旅車，一天的租金是多少？

B It's 50 USD per day without tax. How long will you need the car for?
一天未稅租金是50美金，你要租幾天呢？

A 9 days. I would like to pick it up on September 9 and drop it off on September 17.
九天，我想要九月九號領車，九月十七號還車。

❸ 交通工具篇

B No problem.

沒問題。

延伸例句

▶ What models are available?

你們有哪幾款車?

▶ Would you prefer an automatic or a manual car?

你比較想要自排車還是手排車?

▶ What are your rental rates?

租車的費用怎麼算?

▶ Do you offer unlimited mileage?

有不限哩程數的方案嗎?

▶ Can I return the car to a different location?

我可以在其他地方還車嗎?

▶ Are there any additional charges?

有其他附加費用嗎?

▶ What are the different types of insurance?

你們有哪些不同類型的保險?

▶ Is there a GPS coming with the car?

你們提供衛星導航系統嗎?

▶ What's included in roadside assistance?

道路救援包含什麼服務?

▶ Do I need to return the car with a full tank?
還車的時候必須加滿油嗎？

▶ Please return the car with a full tank of gas.
歸還車子的時候請把油加滿。

▶ How would you like to pay?
你要用甚麼方式付款呢？

▶ Can I pay by debit card?
我可以用金融卡付款嗎？

▶ I'll pay by credit card.
我要刷卡。

▶ I'd like to extend my rental.
我想延長租約。

▶ Do you have an international driver's license?
你有國際駕照嗎？

▶ Are there any particular things I need to know?
有沒有甚麼我特別需要注意的事情呢？

▶ In the event of an accident or emergency, call this toll-free number.
發生意外或緊急情況的話，就打這支免付費電話。

▶ Do you charge extra for an additional driver?
額外駕駛需要多付錢嗎？

▶ What kind of gas does my car take?
我的車加什麼油？

❸ 交通工具篇

▶ What type of gasoline should I use?

我要加哪種油？

▶ Does it require regular or unleaded gas?

要加一般汽油還是無鉛汽油？

相關單字、片語

rent [rɛnt]	租用，租入；租出
kind [kaɪnd]	種類
regular [ˋrɛgjələ]	規則的，有規律的；固定的；正常的；定期的，定時的
sedan [sɪˋdæn]	轎車
SUV (sport utility vehicle)	運動型休旅車
compact [kəmˋpækt]	緊湊的；小巧的；小型的
without [wɪˋðaʊt]	無，沒有，不；在……外面，在……外部
tax [tæks]	稅；稅金
pick up	用汽車搭載某人或接某人；拾起
drop off	讓……下車
model [ˋmɑdl̩]	（汽車等的）型號，樣式
automatic [ˌɔtəˋmætɪk]	自動變速器；自動排檔汽車
manual [ˋmænjʊəl]	手的；手工的；用手操作的
rental [ˋrɛntl̩]	租賃（業）的；供出租的；收取租金的 n. 租金；租金收入；租賃，出租；出租業

unlimited [ʌn`lɪmɪtɪd]	無限制的，無約束的；無數的；無限量的
mileage [`maɪlɪdʒ]	總英里數；行駛哩數
location [lo`keʃən]	位置；場所，所在地
additional [ə`dɪʃən!]	添加的；附加的；額外的
type [taɪp]	類型，型式，樣式
insurance [ɪn`ʃʊrəns]	保險；保險契
GPS (Global Positioning System)	全球（衛星）定位系統
included [ɪn`kludɪd]	被包括的
roadside [`rod͵saɪd]	路邊的，路旁的
assistance [ə`sɪstəns]	援助，幫助
full [fʊl]	滿的；充滿的；吃飽的
tank [tæŋk]	貯水，油，氣等的）櫃，罐，箱，槽；貯水池；池塘
gas [gæs]	汽油
extend [ɪk`stɛnd]	延長，延伸；擴大，擴展
international [͵ɪntə`næʃən!]	國際性的，國際間的
license [`laɪsns]	許可，特許；許可證；執照，牌照
particular [pə`tɪkjələ]	特殊的；特定的；特別的
toll-free [͵tol`fri]	不用付電話費地（的）
gasoline [`gæsə͵lin]	汽油
unleaded [ʌn`lɛdɪd]	不插鉛條的；無鉛的

3.2
巴士、輕軌電車
（購票、搭乘）

會話實例

Ⓐ Can I buy a ticket at the tram stop?
我可以在輕軌電車站買票嗎？

Ⓑ No, there's only a top up machine.
不行，那邊只有加值機器。

Ⓐ Where can I buy a ticket?
我可以去哪買票？

Ⓑ At the train station. It's about 10 minutes walk from here.
在火車站，離這邊走路大概十分鐘。

Ⓐ I see, thank you.
我了解了，謝謝。

Ⓑ By the way, it depends on where you're going. It's free when you travel within zone 1 by tram.
順帶一提，看你要去哪，在區間1內搭輕軌電車旅行都是免費的。

A Oh nice! Thanks for letting me know.

喔太好了！謝謝你跟我說。

B You're welcome.

別客氣。

延伸例句

▶ You can buy a tram card at vending machines or 7-11.

你可以在售票機或 7-11 買電車卡。

▶ You can top up for multiple days.

你可以加值好幾天。

▶ Remember to touch on when you board.

記得在上車時刷卡。

▶ If you don't have a valid ticket when you travel, you may be fincd.

如果你旅行時沒有持有效車票，你可能會被罰款。

▶ Your smart card expired.

你的智慧卡片過期了。

▶ You can download an app called Tram Tracker to see the real-time status.

你可以下載一個叫做 Tram Tracker 的應用程式，可以看到輕軌電車的即時狀況。

▶ Where can I get a bus schedule?

我要去哪裡找巴士時刻表？

❸ 交通工具篇

▶ Which bus goes to the railway station?
請問幾號公車會到火車站？

▶ How often does this bus run?
這班公車班次多久來一次？

▶ Every 15 minutes.
每十五分鐘有一班。

▶ When is the last bus?
末班公車是幾點？

▶ The last bus has left.
末班公車已經離開。

▶ Major tram stations have digital signs that tell you when the next tram is departing.
大型電車站有數位佈告牌讓你知道下班電車幾點出發。

▶ Change is not available. Please use exact change.
不能找錢，請準備正確數量的零錢。

▶ Bus Operators are not allowed to make change for customers.
巴士駕駛員不能找零給客人。

相關單字、片語

top up	加滿；補足
machine [mə`ʃin]	機器；機械
train [tren]	列車，火車
by the way	順便提起；在途中的路邊上
depend [dɪ`pɛnd]	依……而定；取決於
zone [zon]	（鐵路等的）區段；範圍；區域
vending machine	自動販賣機
vend [vɛnd]	出售；販賣
multiple [`mʌltəp!]	由許多部分組成的，複合的；多樣的
remember [rɪ`mɛmbɚ]	記得，記起，記住
touch [tʌtʃ]	觸碰
valid [`vælɪd]	有根據的；確鑿的；令人信服的；合法的；有效的；經正當手續的
fine [faɪn]	處…以罰金
smart [smɑrt]	漂亮的；精明的；聰明
expire [ɪk`spaɪr]	滿期，屆期；（期限）終止；呼氣，吐氣
download [`daʊnˌlod]	下載
real-time	即時的
app	(application的縮寫) 應用程式
often [`ɔfən]	常常，時常；往往，通常
railway [`relˌwe]	鐵路；鐵道
run [rʌn]	（車，船）行駛

sign [saɪn]	標誌；招牌；標牌
exact [ɪgˋzækt]	確切的，精確的； 精確無誤的，精密
operator [ˋɑpəˏretəˋ]	操作者，作業員，技工；司機
allow [əˋlaʊ]	允許，准許
customer [ˋkʌstəməˋ]	顧客；買主

track 35

3.3

地鐵

會話實例

🅐 Excuse me. Could you please tell me which train goes to the Louvre ?
不好意思，請問你可以告訴我哪台列車是去羅浮宮的嗎？

🅑 Sure! You can take the train toward the downtown area to Louvre-Rivoli station.
當然可以！你可以搭乘往市區的列車到羅浮-里沃利站。

🅐 Thank you. Do I need to transfer?
謝謝，我需要中途換車嗎？

B Yes, you will need to transfer at Bastille station.

需要在巴士底站轉車。

A How much is the ticket?

車票要多少錢？

B 4 euros.

4 歐元。

A Here you go.

這邊。

B Thank you. Here's your ticket.

謝謝，這是您的車票。

❸
交通工具篇

延伸例句

▶ I want to buy a one-day pass.
我想要買一日券。

▶ How do I get to the nearest metro?
最近的捷運站怎麼走？

▶ How can I transfer to City hall station?
要如何轉去市政府站？

▶ Which line should I take to go to Shibuya?
我要搭乘哪條線才能去澀谷？

▶ Take the orange line, and then transfer at the green line.
搭乘橘線，然後在綠線轉車。

▶ Which station should I get off?
我要在哪站下車？

▶ Mind the gap between the train and platform.
請留意車廂與月台的縫隙。

相關單字、片語

toward [tə`word]	向，朝；接近，將近
pass [pæs]	通行證；護照；入場證
near [nɪr]	近的；（關係，程度上）接近的；近似的
line [laɪn]	交通線；航線；鐵路線
gap [gæp]	間斷；間隔；間際
between [bɪ`twin]	在……之間

track 36

3.4 火車、高鐵

會話實例

Ⓐ Hi. How may I help you?
嗨，我可以幫忙嗎？

1
2
6

Ⓑ Can I have a ticket to Leeds?
可以給我一張到里茲的車票嗎？

Ⓐ OK. Local train or express train?
好的，你要搭區間車還是特快車？

Ⓑ What is the difference between them?
他們有什麼差別？

Ⓐ The local train stops at every station, while the express train is a non-stop train.
區間車每站都會停，而特快車是直達車。

Ⓑ I see. I'll take the express train.
我了解了，我買特快車。

Ⓐ No problem. The ticket will be 40 pounds. The train will depart at 4 p.m. from platform 2.
沒問題，車票是四十英鎊，火車下午四點從第二月台啟程。

Ⓑ Thank you!
謝謝！

③ 交通工具篇

延伸例句

▶ When is the next train to Edinburgh?
下一班到愛丁堡的火車是幾點？

▶ Hello, one ticket to Birmingham, please.
哈囉，請給我一張到伯明罕的票。

▶ You can book the ticket online 14 days prior to the day of departure.

你可以在啟程日前十四天於網路上訂票。

▶ I bought a high speed rail round-trip ticket online.

我在網路上買了高速鐵路的來回票。

▶ Would you like to travel by first-class or second-class?

請問你要坐頭等車廂還是二等車廂？

▶ What's the price difference between the two classes?

兩種車廂的價格差多少？

▶ Does this train go to London?

這班火車會到倫敦嗎？

▶ Will this train stop at Gold Coast?

這班列車會停黃金海岸嗎？

▶ Does this train stop at every station?

請問這班火車是每站停的嗎？

▶ The next train is leaving in 30 minutes from platform 9.

下班列車在三十分鐘後會從第九月台出發。

▶ Which direction is platform 9?

請問第9月台在哪一個方向？

▶ Are there lockers at Arles station?
亞爾車站有置物箱嗎？

▶ Pardon me. Where is this train heading to?
不好意思，請問這班列車開往哪裡？

▶ Please keep your ticket in case the ticket inspector wants to check it.
請保留車票，以防查票員查票。

▶ Please present your ticket.
請出示您的車票。

▶ This is a C line train, via Garden City, terminating at SunnyBank.
這是C線列車，經由花園城市，終點站為森尼班克。

▶ Only local trains stop at this station.
只有區間車會停這站。

▶ My train is cancelled due to the strike. I'd like to get a refund.
我的火車因為罷工活動取消了，我想要退費。

▶ Due to the strike, all the passengers going to Les Halles please transfer with buses at Nord du Gare station.
因為罷工，所有前往巴黎大堂的乘客請在巴黎北站車站轉乘巴士。

❸
交通工具篇

▶ The trains were delayed for 4 hours due to the flood.
因為淹水，火車誤點四小時。

▶ I missed my train.
我錯過了我的火車。

▶ I think I've taken the wrong train.
我想我坐錯火車了。

▶ You took the wrong direction.
你搭錯方向了。

相關單字、片語

local [ˋlokl]	地方性的；當地的，本地的；鄉土的，狹隘的
express [ɪkˋsprɛs]	快的，直達的；快速行進的，高速的
every [ˋɛvrɪ]	每一，每個；一切的，全部的
online [ˋɑnˏlaɪn]	在網上
prior to	在…之前；首要
prior [ˋpraɪɚ]	在先的
departure [dɪˋpartʃɚ]	離開；出發，起程
high [haɪ]	高的
speed [spid]	速率，速度
rail [rel]	鐵路
round trip	環程旅行；來回旅行

direction [dəˋrɛkʃən]	方向；方位
platform [ˋplætˌfɔrm]	平臺，臺；講臺；（鐵路等的）月臺
pardon me	對不起,請原諒,請再說一遍
ticket inspector	查票員
inspector [ɪnˋspɛktɚ]	檢查員；視察員；督察員；巡官
present [ˋprɛznt]	頒發；出示
via [ˋvaɪə]	經由；取道；透過，憑藉
terminate [ˋtɝməˌnet]	結束；終止
cancel [ˋkænsl̩]	刪去，劃掉，勾銷，蓋銷（郵票等）；取消，廢除；中止
strike [straɪk]	罷工，罷課，罷市
refund [rɪˋfʌnd]	退款金額
due to	因為，由於
wrong [rɔŋ]	錯誤的，不對的

🎧 track 37

3.5 計程車

會話實例

Ⓐ Hello, how are you? I'd like to go to Dubai Marina mall, please.

哈囉，你好嗎？我想要去杜拜港購物中心。

B Hello, sure.

哈囉，好的。

A Can we please pass through Business Bay and pick up my friend on the way?

我們可以在經過商業灣時順便接我的朋友嗎？

B Sure, then I'll have to pass the toll bridge.

好的，但這樣我必須要經過收費橋。

A No problem. Thank you.

沒問題，謝謝。

延伸例句

▶ May I book a taxi at 9 a.m.?

我可以訂早上九點到的計程車嗎？

▶ When will the taxi arrive?

請問計程車什麼時候會到？

▶ Excuse me, could you hail a taxi for me please?

不好意思，可以麻煩你幫我叫計程車嗎？

▶ I'm at No.6, Oak Street.

我在橡木街六號。

▶ Could you send the taxi to Abraj al Mamzar Building?

可以請計程車到Abraj al Mamzar大樓嗎？

▶ Could you take me to Pullman airport hotel?
可以麻煩你載我去Pullman機場飯店嗎？

▶ I'd like to go to Centre Pompidou.
我想要去龐畢度中心。

▶ Can you avoid toll roads?
你可以避開收費路段嗎？

▶ How much will that cost?
這樣是多少錢？

▶ Do you use the meter?
你是照跳錶收費嗎？

▶ How much is the fare, please?
要多少錢？

▶ How much do I owe you?
我要付你多少錢？

▶ I'm really in a hurry, can you take the fastest route, please?
我真的很趕，可以請你走最快的路嗎？

▶ Can we pass through the Geneva water fountain on the way?
我們沿途可以經過日內瓦大噴泉嗎？

▶ Keep the change.
不用找零。

旅遊英文 一點通

相關單字、片語

marina [mə`rinə]	小艇碼頭；小艇船塢
mall [mɔl]	購物中心
pass through	通過，穿過；經歷，經驗
toll [tol]	（路，橋等的）通行費； 使用費；服務費
on the way	正在去的路上
bridge [brɪdʒ]	橋，橋樑
arrive [ə`raɪv]	到達；到來
hail [hel]	招呼
street [strit]	街，街道
avoid [ə`vɔɪd]	避開，躲開；避免
road [rod]	路，道路，公路；街道，馬路
cost [kɔst]	費用；成本
meter [`mitɚ]	計量器，儀表
fare [fɛr]	交通工具的）票價，車（船）
owe [o]	欠（債等）
fast [fæst]	快的；迅速的；速度快的； 完成得快的
route [rut]	路；路線；路程；航線
fountain [`fauntɪn]	泉水；噴泉；水源； 人造噴泉；噴水池

①
③
④

3.6

公共腳踏車、電動滑板車

會話實例

🅐 Have you tried those electric scooters?

你有嘗試過那些電動滑板車嗎？

🅑 Yea, it's fun to ride.

有的，很好玩。

🅐 How do you use them?

要怎麼使用？

🅑 Download their app. There you can create a profile, add a phone number, your card details to pay and you're good to go.

下載應用程式，在上面建立個人檔案，加入手機號碼、你的卡片資料以便付款，然後就可以使用了。

🅐 Can I ride them on the street?

我可以騎在馬路上嗎？

🅑 Technically, riders are supposed to use the sidewalk.

嚴格來說，騎士應該要使用人行道。

③
交通工具篇

A Ah, I see. Can I return them to another location?

阿，我了解了。我可以在別的地點歸還嗎？

B Yes, You can park it at a different designated parking space.

可以，你可以停在別的指定停放區。

延伸例句

▶ You can rent it by using a smartphone app.
你可以透過智慧型手機應用程式租借。

▶ The map shows you where available scooters are.
地圖會告訴你哪裡有電動車。

▶ You can rent a bike directly from a kiosk with your credit card or contactless payment.
你可以從腳踏車亭直接用信用卡或無接觸式付款租借腳踏車。

▶ Swipe your card when returning the bike, the system will automatically charge the fees.
還腳踏車時刷卡，系統會自動扣款。

▶ The public bicycles make getting around the city easier and more accessible.
公共自行車讓人們能夠更輕鬆、方便地在城市四處遊歷。

相關單字、片語

electric [ɪˋlɛktrɪk]	電的;導電的;發電的;用電的;電動的
scooter [ˋskutɚ]	速克達(一種小型摩托車);(兒童遊戲用的)踏板車
ride [raɪd]	騎馬,乘車;騎馬(或乘車)旅行
create [krɪˋet]	創造;創作;設計;創建;創設
profile [ˋprofaɪl]	傳略,人物簡介;概況
add [æd]	添加;增加
detail [ˋditel]	細節;詳情;瑣事;枝節
pay [pe]	付,支付;付款給
technically [ˋtɛknɪkḷɪ]	技術上;工藝上;技巧上;嚴密地來說;嚴格按照法律地
rider [ˋraɪdɚ]	騎馬(或騎腳踏車等的)人;搭乘的人
supposed to	應該,可以
sidewalk [ˋsaɪd͵wɔk]	人行道
park [pɑrk]	停放(車輛等)
designate [ˋdɛzɪg͵net]	標出;表明;指定;把……定名為,稱呼
space [spes]	空間
smartphone	智慧型手機;智能手機
map [mæp]	地圖;天體圖
bike [baɪk]	腳踏車;摩托車

directly [də`rɛktlɪ]	直接地；筆直地；坦率地，直截了當地
kiosk [kɪ`ɑsk]	（土耳其等地的）涼亭；（亭式的）公用電話亭，報攤
contactless payment	非接觸式支付
contactless ['kɒn.tækt.ləs]	不接觸的；無接點的；遙控的；感應式的
payment [`pemənt]	支付，付款
swipe [swaɪp]	揮擊；猛擊；碰擦，擦過；刷（卡）；（手指在螢幕上）滑動
system [`sɪstəm]	體系；系統
public [`pʌblɪk]	公眾的；公共的，公用的
bicycle [`baɪsɪk!]	腳踏車，自行車
get around	各處旅行，廣泛遊歷
easy [`izɪ]	容易的；不費力的
accessible [æk`sɛsəb!]	可（或易）接近的；可（或易）進入的；可（或易）得到的；可（或易）使用的

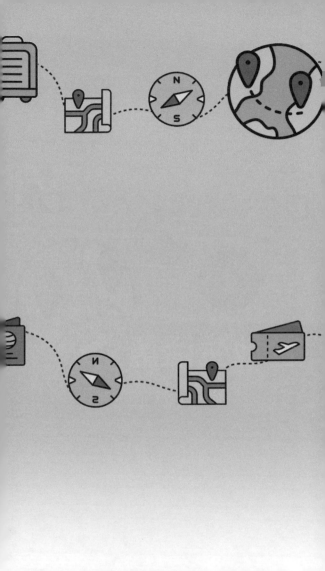

4

當地生活篇

談論天氣
（下雨、下雪）

會話實例

A How's the weather out there?
外面的天氣如何？

B It's freezing!
超級冷！

A Is it raining?
有下雨嗎？

B No, but I think it's about to rain, you better bring an umbrella.
沒有，但我覺得看起來快下雨了，你最好帶雨傘。

A Alright, thanks.
沒問題，謝啦。

B Don't forget to bring a jacket, too.
也別忘了帶件外套。

A Ok, mom.
好的，媽。

4 當地生活篇

延伸例句

▶ What's it like out there?
外面的天氣如何？

▶ What's the weather like out there?
外面的天氣如何？

▶ What's the temperature like?
外面的氣溫如何？

▶ What's the weather forecast?
天氣預報是怎樣？

▶ It's been drizzling all day.
濛濛細雨下了一整天。

▶ Some showers are expected today.
今天將有陣雨。

▶ It's raining cats and dogs!
現在正下著傾盆大雨！

▶ My clothes are a little wet because of the rain.
因為下雨，我的衣服有點濕。

▶ It's going to rain soon.
即將要下雨了。

▶ It looks like rain.
要下雨了。

▶ The rain has stopped.

雨停了。

▶ We have to cancel the basketball match because of the rain.

因為下雨，我們必須取消籃球比賽。

▶ Afternoon thunderstorms are frequent during summer in Singapore.

午後雷陣雨在新加坡夏日很常發生。

▶ There's a rainbow in the sky.

天空有一道彩虹。

▶ The sky grew dark and it started to thunder.

天色變暗，開始打雷了。

▶ There's a storm brewing.

有一場暴風雨正在醞釀。

▶ It's a bit chilly.

有點冷。

▶ It's extremely cold out there.

外面冷死了。

▶ We couldn't play badminton because it was too windy.

我們不能打羽毛球，因為風太大了。

▶ It's has been hailing for 30 minutes.

冰雹下了三十分鐘。

❹ 當地生活篇

▶ It's snowing.
下雪了。

▶ There will be snow this Sunday.
星期天會下雪。

▶ When will it stop snowing?
雪什麼時候會停？

▶ It will be below freezing for most of the day.
今天大部份時間都會是零度以下。

▶ Everyone driving should monitor the forecast and expect to drive at slower speeds when the snow is falling.
下雪的時候，所有駕駛都應該要掌控氣象預報並且有放慢速度行駛的準備。

相關單字、片語

weather [ˋwɛðɚ]	天氣
freezing [ˋfrizɪŋ]	凍結的；冰凍的；極冷的
rain [ren]	下雨，降雨
umbrella [ʌmˋbrɛlə]	傘，雨傘；保護傘，庇護
alright [ˋɔlˋraɪt]	沒問題地（的），健康地（的）；極好地（的）
out [aʊt]	出外；在外
temperature [ˋtɛmprətʃɚ]	溫度，氣溫
forecast [ˋforˏkæst]	預測，預報

drizzle [ˈdrɪz!]	下毛毛雨
shower [ˈʃaʊɚ]	陣雨；冰雹
expect [ɪkˈspɛkt]	預計……可能發生（或來到）；預料；預期；期待
clothes [kloz]	衣服；服裝
wet [wɛt]	濕的，潮濕的
soon [sun]	不久，很快地；快，早
basketball [ˈbæskɪtˌbɔl]	籃球運動
match [mætʃ]	比賽，競賽；對手
thunderstorm [ˈθʌndɚˌstɔrm]	大雷雨
frequent [ˈfrikwənt]	時常發生的，頻繁的；屢次的；慣常的；習以為常的
rainbow [ˈrenˌbo]	虹，彩虹
sky [skaɪ]	天，天空
grow [gro]	成長，生長；發育；增大，增加；發展
dark [dɑrk]	暗；黑暗的；（顏色）深的
thunder [ˈθʌndɚ]	打雷；發出雷鳴般響聲
storm [stɔrm]	暴風雨
brew [bru]	圖謀，策劃；醞釀
a bit	稍微，有一點兒；短時間，短距離
chilly [ˈtʃɪlɪ]	冷颼颼的；冷得使人不舒服的；怕冷的
play [ple]	打（球）
badminton [ˈbædmɪntən]	羽毛球

④ 當地生活篇

extremely [ɪkˋstrimlɪ]	極端地;極其;非常
windy [ˋwɪndɪ]	刮風的;多風的;風大的;受風的
hail [hel]	下冰雹
snow [sno]	vi. 下雪;雪片似地落下 n. 雪
below [bəˋlo]	在下面;到下面;在下方
monitor [ˋmɑnətɚ]	監控;監聽;監測;監視
slow [slo]	慢的,緩緩的;遲緩的;費事的,耗時的
fall [fɔl]	落下;跌倒

🎧 track 40

4.2 談論天氣(晴天)

會話實例

Ⓐ Good morning!
早安!

Ⓑ Good morning!
早安!

Ⓐ Wow! It finally cleared up!
哇!終於放晴了!

Ⓑ Isn't it great?
是不是很棒?

A What a beautiful day! Let's go picnicking in the woods.

今天天氣很好！我們去森林裡野餐吧。

B Ok, I'll go wake up the kids.

好呀，我來叫孩子起床。

A I'll make us some sandwiches.

我來幫大家做三明治。

B Great!

太好了！

延伸例句

▶ It's sunny and hot.
出大太陽而且很熱。

▶ It'll clear up in the afternoon.
下午會放晴。

▶ The sun is shining outside.
外面豔陽高照。

▶ The sky is crystal clear after a week of heavy rain and storms.
在一週的大雨及暴風雨後，現在天空清澈晴朗。

▶ The sky is quite blue.
天空很蔚藍。

▶ The sky is bright.
天空晴朗。

❹ 當地生活篇

▶ The weather is suitable for sunbathing.
這種天氣很適合曬太陽。

▶ Let's go to the beach and enjoy the sunshine!
我們去海邊享受陽光！

▶ What a lovely day!
今天天氣好好！

▶ Sunshine will be back in full this afternoon.
天空今天下午將會全面恢復晴朗。

相關單字、片語

finally [ˋfaɪn!ɪ]	最後，終於；決定性地
clear up	放晴
clear [klɪr]	vi. 變乾淨；變清澈；變晴；變清楚 adj. 清澈的，透明的；（皮膚）潔淨的；明亮的；晴朗的
beautiful [ˋbjutəfəl]	美麗的，漂亮的；出色的，完美的
picnic [ˋpɪknɪk]	（自帶食物的）郊遊，野餐
woods [wʊdz]	樹林；森林
kid [kɪd]	小孩
sandwich [ˋsændwɪtʃ]	三明治；三明治狀物
sunny [ˋsʌnɪ]	陽光充足的；和煦的，暖和的
hot [hɑt]	熱
shine [ʃaɪn]	發光；照耀；顯露；發亮

crystal [ˋkrɪstḷ]	水晶的，水晶製的；水晶般的，清澈的，透明的
week [wik]	週，一星期；工作日，上課日，普通日
bright [braɪt]	明亮的；發亮的；晴朗的
suitable [ˋsutəbḷ]	適當的；合適的；適宜的
sunbathe [ˋsʌn͵beð]	沐日光浴
enjoy [ɪnˋdʒɔɪ]	欣賞；享受；喜愛
sunshine [ˋsʌn͵ʃaɪn]	陽光；晴天
back [bæk]	回覆；還；往回

🎧 track 41

4.3 談論天氣（溫暖、炎熱天氣）

會話實例

Ⓐ Hello, Diana, it's Jamie.

哈囉，黛安娜，是我潔咪。

Ⓑ Hi, Jamie. How are you?

嗨，潔咪，你好嗎？

Ⓐ I'm good, thanks. How's the weather there today?

我很好，謝謝，你們那邊今天天氣如何？

B It's burning hot!
超級熱！

A What's the temperature?
氣溫幾度？

B It's about 42°C.
大概攝氏四十二度。

A Wow! That's terrible!
哇！真可怕！

B Yea, it's better for me to stay indoors.
對呀，我最好待在室內。

延伸例句

▶ I love warm weather, that's why I moved to the south.
我喜歡溫暖的天氣，這是我搬去南部的原因。

▶ I feel very hot.
我覺得很熱。

▶ It's baking hot!
熱得像在火爐中烤似的！

▶ It's boiling hot.
非常熱。

▶ The heat is unbearable.
酷熱的天氣令人難以忍受。

▶ The hot weather makes me sweat a lot.
　炎熱的天氣讓我滿頭大汗。

相關單字、片語

burning [ˋbɝnɪŋ]	燃燒的，著火的；發熱的；火熱的
terrible [ˋtɛrəbḷ]	可怕的，嚇人的，可怖的；極度的，嚴重的
indoors [ˋɪnˋdorz]	在室內，在屋裡；往室內
baking [ˋbeɪkɪŋ]	酷熱的
boiling [ˋbɔɪlɪŋ]	沸騰的；激昂的
heat [hit]	熱度；溫度；暑熱；高溫
unbearable [ʌnˋbɛrəbḷ]	不能忍受的；令人不能容忍的
sweat [swɛt]	汗，汗水

❹當地生活篇

談論天氣（其他天氣）

會話實例

Ⓐ Hey. This is John calling. How's it going?
嘿，我是約翰，還好嗎？

Ⓑ I'm good, thanks.
我很好，謝謝。

Ⓐ I saw the news, the approaching typhoon will be strong.
我看到新聞報導說正在逼近的颱風是強烈颱風。

Ⓑ Yes. The government in Taiwan has declared tomorrow a typhoon day.
對，台灣縣市政府已宣布明天放颱風假。

Ⓐ Did you stock up on some food?
你有儲備一些糧食嗎？

Ⓑ Yes, I went to the supermarket this afternoon. The shelves were half empty.
我下午去超市，架上都空了一半。

Ⓐ That's crazy. Alright, take care!
真瘋狂，好吧，小心點！

B I will. Thank you!
我會的，謝謝。

延伸例句

▶ The wind is so strong today.
今天風好大。

▶ All flights and trains were cancelled due to the typhoon.
因為颱風，所有班機和火車班次都被取消了。

▶ The Central Weather Bureau issued a sea warning.
中央氣象局發布颱風警報。

▶ The typhoon caused severe flooding in the northern Philippines.
颱風在菲律賓北部造成嚴重的水災。

▶ The flood washed out the bridge.
洪水把橋樑沖走了。

▶ I didn't go out because of the sandstorm.
因為沙塵暴，我沒有外出。

▶ A hurricane is coming.
颶風就要來了。

相關單字、片語

news [njuz]	新聞;消息;報導
approach [əˋprotʃɪŋ]	將近;近乎,即將達到
typhoon [taɪˋfun]	颱風
strong [strɔŋ]	強壯的,強健的;強大的
government [ˋgʌvɚnmənt]	政府,內閣
stock up	(為某種需要或目的)儲備(某物)
food [fud]	食物,食品
supermarket [ˋsupɚͺmarkɪt]	超級市場
shelf [ʃɛlf]	架子;擱板;架子(或擱板)上的東西
half [hæf]	一半,二分之一
empty [ˋɛmptɪ]	空的;未佔用的;無人居住的;無,沒有,缺少
crazy [ˋkrezɪ]	瘋狂的
take care	小心;當心;注意
bureau [ˋbjʊro]	局,司,署,處
issue [ˋɪʃʊ]	發行;發布;發給,配給
warning [ˋwɔrnɪŋ]	警告;告誡;警報
cause [kɔz]	導致,使發生,引起
flooding [ˋflʌdɪŋ]	泛濫
flood [flʌd]	洪水,水災
northern [ˋnɔrðɚn]	北方的;向北方的
wash out	沖走;被沖走;沖毀
sandstorm [ˋsændͺstɔrm]	大風沙;沙暴
hurricane [ˋhɝͺken]	颶風,暴風雨

4.5 租房

會話實例

A Hello, I saw your rental advertisement in the newspaper. I'm looking for a studio. Is it still available?

哈囉,我看到您在報紙上刊登的租房廣告,我正在找一個套房,請問還有空房嗎?

B Hello, thank you for calling. Yes, it's available.

哈囉,謝謝您的來電,是的,還有空房喔。

A Is it furnished?

請問有附傢俱嗎?

B Yes, it's equipped with a refrigerator, gas cooker, TV, air conditioner, bed, dining table and washing machine.

有的,有提供冰箱、瓦斯爐、電視、冷氣、床、餐桌跟洗衣機。

A Does the rent include the utilities?

租金有包含水電費嗎?

B Yes, it's included.

有的,含水電。

4 當地生活篇

A Great! When can I visit the apartment?

太棒了！請問何時方便讓我去看房呢？

B I'm available from Monday to Friday, 13 pm to 9 pm.

我星期一到星期五，下午一點到晚上九點都可以。

延伸例句

▶ I'm looking for a two-bedroom apartment.

我在找兩間房的公寓。

▶ How much is the rent per month?

請問月租費是多少元？

▶ What is the minimum length for the lease?

請問這間房間最短租約是多久？

▶ What is the duration of the lease?

請問要簽約要簽多久呢？

▶ Do I have to pay a deposit?

我要付押金嗎？

▶ How much is the security deposit?

押金多少？

▶ Fully furnished or partly furnished?

齊全的傢俱還是只有部分傢俱？

▶ When can I move in?

請問何時我可以搬入？

▶ Are there laundry facilities?
請問有洗衣機等設備嗎？

▶ Are pets allowed in this building?
請問可以養寵物嗎？

▶ What furniture do you provide?
有提供什麼傢俱？

▶ Is there a dishwasher in the kitchen?
廚房裡有洗碗機嗎？

▶ Is there a security system?
有保全系統嗎？

▶ Any rules for the tenant?
有什麼住戶規定嗎？

▶ Should I pay all at once?
我需要一次付清嗎？

▶ When do I pay the rent?
請問什麼時候要付房租呢？

▶ Is the metro station within walking distance?
請問捷運站走路走得到嗎？

▶ How far is it from the bus stop?
距離公車站有多遠？

❹ 當地生活篇

旅遊英文一點通

相關單字、片語

advertisement [ˌædvəˋtaɪzmənt]	廣告，宣傳
newspaper [ˋnjuzˌpepə]	報紙，報
studio [ˋstjudɪo]	單房公寓（通常一個房間兼作睡房和起居室，帶有廁所，有的有單獨的廚房）
still [stɪl]	還，仍舊；儘管如此，然而
furnish [ˋfɜnɪʃ]	給（房間）配置（傢俱等）；裝備[（+with）]；供應；提供
equip [ɪˋkwɪp]	裝備，配備
gas cooker	瓦斯爐；燃氣爐；燃氣灶
air conditioner	空氣調節裝置；冷氣機
conditioner [kənˋdɪʃənə]	調節器
dining [ˋdaɪnɪŋ]	進餐
table [ˋtebl]	桌子；餐桌
washing [ˋwɑʃɪŋ]	洗，洗滌
include [ɪnˋklud]	包括，包含
apartment [əˋpɑrtmənt]	（一戶）公寓房間
minimum [ˋmɪnəməm]	最小量，最小數；最低限度
length [lɛŋθ]	長度；（時間的）長短，期間
lease [lis]	租約，租契；租賃；租賃權
duration [djʊˋreʃən]	持續，持久；持續期間
deposit [dɪˋpɑzɪt]	保證金；押金；定金
fully [ˋfʊlɪ]	完全地；徹底地；充分地
partly [ˋpɑrtlɪ]	部分地；不完全地
laundry [ˋlɔndrɪ]	洗衣店，洗衣房
facility [fəˋsɪlətɪ]	（供特定用途的）場所

1
5
8

pet [pɛt]	供玩賞的動物，寵物
building [ˋbɪldɪŋ]	建築物，房屋
furniture [ˋfɝnɪtʃɚ]	傢俱
dishwasher [ˋdɪʃˌwaʃɚ]	洗碗機
security [sɪˋkjʊrətɪ]	防備，保安
rule [rul]	規則，規定
tenant [ˋtɛnənt]	房客
at once	立刻，馬上，即
walking [ˋwɔkɪŋ]	走；步行
distance [ˋdɪstəns]	距離；路程

 track 44

4.6 租房後遇到的問題

會話實例

Ⓐ Hello, how can I help you?
哈囉，你需要幫忙嗎？

Ⓑ Hey, do you have a minute?
嘿，你有時間嗎？

Ⓐ Yes.
有。

❹ 當地生活篇

B There is a water leak in my apartment. Would you send the maintenance staff to come and check?

我的公寓裡有漏水問題，可以麻煩你請維修人員來檢查嗎？

A Sure, Are you available today?

當然，你今天有空嗎？

B Yes, I'll be home all day.

有的，我今天整天會在家。

A I'll send them right away.

我請他們馬上過去。

B Thank you very much!

非常感謝你！

延伸例句

▶ The washing machine isn't working. Could you please send someone to fix it?

洗衣機壞掉了，可以請你請人來修理嗎？

▶ Who is responsible for the building's maintenance?

誰負責這座大樓的保養事宜？

▶ The doorknob is loose.

門的握把鬆了。

▶ It is difficult to unlock the door.
門鎖很難打開。

▶ It's difficult to get the key into the lock.
鑰匙很難插進門鎖裡。

▶ The door lock is jammed.
門卡住了。

▶ I can't access the wifi.
我無法連上網路。

▶ There's no internet connection. Could you help me to check it?
現在沒有網路，可以幫我確認是什麼狀況嗎？

▶ The neighbor on the third floor always leaves their garbage in the hallway which leaves an unpleasant smell.
三樓的鄰居總是把垃圾堆在走廊，味道很難聞。

▶ I'm sorry but I have to complain about the neighbors upstairs. They are very noisy.
不好意思，但是我必須投訴樓上的鄰居。他們太吵了。

▶ Could you tell them to lower their voices?
能請你幫我告知他們嗎？

❹ 當地生活篇

▶ The circuit breaker has tripped. How can I fix it?

跳電了,請問要怎麼修復它?

相關單字、片語

minute [ˋmɪnɪt]	分(鐘)
leak [lik]	(水,瓦斯等的)漏出
maintenance staff	維修人員
maintenance [ˋmentənəns]	維修,保養
staff [stæf]	職員,工作人員
fix [fɪks]	修理;校準
responsible [rɪˋspɑnsəb!]	需負責任的,承擔責任的
doorknob [ˋdor͵nɑb]	球形門拉手
loose [lus]	鬆的,寬的;鬆散的
unlock [ʌnˋlɑk]	開……的鎖;開;開啟
lock [lɑk]	鎖
jam [dʒæm]	塞緊;擠滿;堵塞;卡住,不能動彈;發生故障
access [ˋæksɛs]	存取(資料);使用;接近
Internet [ˋɪntɚ͵nɛt]	網際網路
connection [kəˋnɛkʃən]	連接;聯絡;銜接
neighbor [ˋnebɚ]	鄰居
always [ˋɔlwɛz]	總是,經常
garbage [ˋgɑrbɪdʒ]	垃圾;剩菜
hallway [ˋhɔl͵we]	玄關;門廳

unpleasant [ʌn`plɛznt]	使人不愉快的；不中意的；討厭的
smell [smɛl]	氣味；香味
complain [kəm`plen]	控訴，投訴
upstairs [`ʌp`stɛrz]	在樓上；往樓上
noisy [`nɔɪzɪ]	喧鬧的，嘈雜的
lower [`loə]	放下，降下；放低
voice [vɔɪs]	聲音；嗓子
circuit breaker	斷路器，斷路開關
circuit [`sɝkɪt]	電路；回路；線路圖
trip trɪp]	絆，絆倒；使失誤

🎧 track 45

4.7 申辦網路、電話

會話實例

🅐 Hello. How may I help you?
哈囉，需要幫忙嗎？

🅑 Hi, I'd like to know about your home internet plans.
嗨，我想要知道你們的家庭網路方案。

🅐 What kind of services are you looking for?
你需要什麼樣的服務？

B I'm looking for high speed internet, TV and calls.

我想要高速網路、電視跟通話。

A We have 3 different plans with broadband speeds ranging from 1Gbps, 500Mbps and 300Mbps.

我們有三種不同的寬頻網路方案，1Gbps, 500Mbps 和 300Mbps。

B What are the prices?

價格各是多少呢？

A Respectively : 80 USD, 60 USD and 40 USD.

分別是80、60和40美元。

B How long is the subscription for ?

合約是多久？

A 2 years.

兩年。

延伸例句

▶ I'd like to know about your mobile phone plans.
我想知道你們的手機方案。

▶ What is included in each plan?
每個方案各包含什麼？

▶ What's the monthly fee?
月費是多少？

▶ I'd like to buy a prepaid mobile SIM card.
我想要買手機儲值卡。

▶ Are you looking for a monthly plan?
你在尋找月租方案嗎？

▶ How do I keep track of my usage?
我要怎麼看使用流量。

▶ How can I recharge my prepaid service?
我要如何儲值預付服務？

▶ You can recharge, check your balance and manage your usage on the app.
你可以使用手機應用程式儲值、查詢餘額還有控制流量。

▶ Would you like to change your existing prepaid plan?
您想要改變現有的預付方案嗎？

▶ Can I keep my number when switching plan?
變更方案可以保留原本的電話號碼嗎？

▶ How long does it take to transfer my number?
轉移門號要多久時間？

▶ Is there a cost to transfer my number?
轉移門號要付費嗎？

❹ 當地生活篇

旅遊英文 一點通

▶ How long does it take to deliver my order?
我的訂單多久後會寄達？

▶ How can I activate my prepaid SIM?
我要如何啟動預付卡？

▶ Can I cancel my subscription anytime?
我可以隨時取消訂閱嗎？

▶ How do I change plans?
要如何更改方案？

▶ What destinations can I call if I have a standard plan including unlimited international calls?
若是我使用無限國際電話標準方案，有哪些地點是我可以撥打的？

▶ Can I make calls to these international destinations from anywhere?
我能夠從任何地方撥打到這些國外地點嗎？

▶ What happens if I go over my plan's included data?
如果我使用超過方案限制的流量會怎麼樣？

▶ All services on your account will continue to use data at maximum speeds of up to 1.5Mbps.
您可以繼續使用所有在您的帳戶上的服務，最高網速為 1.5Mbps。

▶ How fast is your 5G home internet?
你們的 5G 家用網路有多快？

▶ I want to buy data roaming.
我想要購買國際漫遊。

▶ I'd like to top up for date roaming.
我想要加值國際漫遊。

▶ I want to buy mobile phone insurance.
我想要購買手機保險。

▶ How much does it cost and what does it cover?
要多少錢，有包含什麼？

相關單字、片語

plan [plæn]	計畫；方案；打算
broadband [`brɔd`bænd]	多頻率的
respectively [rɪ`spɛktɪvlɪ]	分別地，各自地
subscription [səb`skrɪpʃən]	預訂；訂閱；會費
mobile [`mobɪl]	可動的，移動式的，活動的
mobile phone	行動電話，便攜電話
each [itʃ]	兩個或兩個以上人或物中的) 各；各自的；每
monthly [`mʌnθlɪ]	每月的；每月一次的
prepaid [pri`ped]	預先付的；已付的
keep track of	了解...的動態(或線索)；記錄
track [træk]	行蹤；軌道

❹ 當地生活篇

usage [ˋjusɪdʒ]	使用，用法；處理
recharge [riˋtʃɑrdʒ]	再充電於；再裝填彈藥
balance [ˋbæləns]	結存；結餘
manage [ˋmænɪdʒ]	管理；經營
existing [ɪgˋzɪstɪŋ]	現存的；現行的
switch [swɪtʃ]	變更，轉換，更改
deliver [dɪˋlɪvɚ]	投遞；傳送；運送
order [ˋɔrdɚ]	訂購；訂貨；訂單
activate [ˋæktəˌvet]	啟動；觸發；使活化
anytime [ˋɛnɪˌtaɪm]	在任何時候；總是，無例外地；一定
standard [ˋstændɚd]	標準的
anywhere [ˋɛnɪˌhwɛr]	在任何地方
data [ˋdetə]	資料，數據；datum的名詞複數
account [əˋkaunt]	帳戶；客戶
maximum [ˋmæksəməm]	最大量，最大數，最大限度
roaming	國際漫遊
roam [rom]	漫步；漫遊；流浪
cover [ˋkʌvɚ]	包含；適用於

4.8 去銀行

會話實例

Ⓐ Hello, I'd like to open a bank account. What are the options?

哈囉,我想要開立銀行帳戶,請問有哪些選擇?

Ⓑ For personal accounts, we have checking and saving accounts.

我們有活期存款及儲蓄這兩種個人帳戶。

Ⓐ Are there any fees?

要付費嗎?

Ⓑ No, there are no monthly or application fees.

不用,不需要月費或申請費。

Ⓐ That's great. Can I open both?

太好了,我可以兩個都開嗎?

Ⓑ Yes, sure. May I have your passport, please?

可以,請給我您的護照。

Ⓐ Here you go.

給你。

❹ 當地生活篇

B Would you like to apply for a VISA debit card?

你想要申請金融信用卡嗎？

延伸例句

▷ There are no minimum deposits.
沒有最低存款規定。

▷ With our platinum credit card, you get 1% cash back on any purchase.
我們的白金信用卡提供您1%的現金回饋，不限消費種類。

▷ I'd like to make a deposit.
我想要存款。

▷ I'd like to withdraw 5000 USD.
我想要提領5000美元。

▷ I'm going to travel, can I withdraw money at the ATM overseas with this card?
我即將出國旅行，這張卡可以在國外ATM提款嗎？

▷ I'd like to get a credit card.
我想要申請信用卡。

▷ I'd like to apply for a personal loan.
我想要申辦個人貸款。

▷ How to register for internet banking?
要如何註冊網路銀行？

▶ Please enter your ID number.
請輸入您的身份證號碼。

▶ Please create a password.
請設定密碼。

▶ Please enter your personal details.
請輸入您的個人資料。

▶ I'd like to deposit a check.
我想要兌換支票。

▶ I forgot my PIN number.
我忘記我的個人識別碼。

▶ I had my credit card stolen.
我的信用卡被偷了。

▶ My debit card is missing.
我的金融卡不見了。

▶ My wallet is stolen, I'm calling to report a stolen card.
我的錢包被偷了，我打來掛失信用卡。

▶ May I have your passbook?
可以給我您的存摺嗎？

▶ Please sign on this slip.
請在這張紙條簽名。

▶ Please fill out this form and sign here.
請填這張表格並在這簽名。

❹ 當地生活篇

▶ I would like to deposit my paycheck into my savings account.
  我想要把薪資支票存到我的儲蓄帳戶。

▶ I'd like to wire transfer money overseas.
  我要電匯一筆錢到國外。

▶ We have free online banking.
  我們有提供免費的線上銀行服務。

▶ You can pay all your bills and manage your accounts over the Internet.
  您可以線上支付帳單或管理您的帳戶。

▶ You can change your password at the ATM.
  您可以在ATM更換密碼。

▶ I want to close my account.
  我想關閉帳戶。

相關單字、片語

open [`opən]	開；打開
personal [`pɝsn!]	個人的，私人的
saving [`sevɪŋ]	儲金，存款，儲蓄額
deposit [dɪ`pazɪt]	存款
platinum [`plætnəm]	鉑，白金
purchase [`pɝtʃəs]	n. 買，購

ATM = Automated Teller Machine, Automatic Teller Machine	自動存提款機
withdraw [wɪð`drɔ]	取回；提取
overseas [`ovɚ`siz]	在（或向）海外； 在（或向）國外
loan [lon]	貸款
banking [`bæŋkɪŋ]	銀行業務
enter [`ɛntɚ]	登錄；將……輸入
create [krɪ`et]	創建；創設
password [`pæs,wɝd]	密碼
pin = personal identification number 個人識別碼	
steal [stil]	偷，竊取
wallet [`wɑlɪt]	皮夾子，錢包
passbook [`pæs,bʊk]	存款簿；銀行存摺
slip [slɪp]	片條，板條；紙條
paycheck [`pe,tʃɛk]	付薪水的支票；薪津
wire transfer [`waɪər trænsfɚ] 電匯	
close [klos]	關閉；蓋上；結束

track 47

4.9 郵寄包裹

會話實例

Ⓐ I'd like to send this parcel to France. What are the options?

我想要寄這個包裹到法國。請問有什麼選擇？

Ⓑ We have Economy, Standard and Express delivery.

我們有經濟郵件、標準郵件及快捷郵件。

Ⓐ What are the prices?

價格各是多少？

Ⓑ Which city?

要寄到哪個城市？

Ⓐ Nice.

尼斯。

Ⓑ Please put your parcel on the scale.

請把你的包裹放到秤子上。

Ⓐ Sure.

好的。

B It's 20 AUD for Economy, 27 AUD for Standard and 43 AUD for Express.

經濟郵件20澳幣、標準郵件27澳幣、快捷郵件43澳幣。

延伸例句

▶ What are the different domestic delivery services?

有哪些不同的國內寄送服務？

▶ What's the postage?

郵資是多少？

▶ How much does it cost to send this letter to Poland by EMS?

請問用快捷郵件寄這封信到波蘭要多少？

▶ How long will it take to arrive?

多久會到達？

▶ It'll take about 5-7 days.

大約五到七天。

▶ What are the maximum parcel size and weight that we can send abroad?

國際包裹的最大尺寸及重量是多少？

▶ Are there any restrictions on the goods I'm sending to an international destination?

我要寄商品到國外，有任何限制規定嗎？

❹ 當地生活篇

▶ I want to send the parcel by airmail to Italy.
我想要空運包裹到義大利。

▶ Airmail or surface mail？
航空還是普通郵件。

▶ Would you like regular or express delivery?
要寄普通還是限時呢？

▶ Can I track this delivery?
我可以追蹤這個郵件嗎？

▶ Where do I find my tracking number?
我要在哪裡可以找到我的追蹤號碼？

▶ How do I track my item?
我要如何追蹤我的物品？

▶ What's inside the parcel?
包裹裡面是裝什麼？

▶ There are 3 glasses inside.
裡面有三個玻璃杯。

▶ Did you pack them properly?
你有包裝好嗎？

▶ Please fill out this form.
請填寫這個寄送單。

▶ I'd like to buy prepaid satchels.
我想要買預付便利袋。

▶ I'd like to pick up my certified mail.
我想要領取掛號信。

▶ I'd like to send the letter by certified mail.
我想用掛號寄這封信。

▶ I'd like to buy 5 stamps.
我想要買五張郵票。

▶ What travel insurance plans do you have?
你們有哪些旅遊保險方案？

▶ Where is the closest parcel locker around here?
最近的包裹置物櫃在哪裡？

▶ Do you offer parcel insurance?
你們有提供包裹保險嗎？

▶ Please don't forget to put a return address on the envelope.
請別忘記在信封上寫上寄件人的地址。

❹ 當地生活篇

相關單字、片語

parcel [ˈpɑrsl]	小包，包裹
domestic [dəˈmɛstɪk]	國家的；國內的
postage [ˈpostɪdʒ]	郵資，郵費
size [saɪz]	尺寸，大小
weight [wet]	重，重量
restriction [rɪˈstrɪkʃən]	限制；約束

goods [gʊdz]	商品;貨物;動
surface [`sɝ·fɪs]	(郵件)陸路的,普通的,水路的
airmail [`ɛrˌmel]	航空郵件;航空信
inside [`ɪn`saɪd]	在……的裡面
glass [glæs]	玻璃杯
satchel [`sætʃəl]	書包;小背包
certified mail	掛號信
certified [`sɝ·təˌfaɪd]	被證明的;有保證的;公認的
stamp [stæmp]	郵票;印花
address [ə`drɛs]	住址,地址
envelope [`ɛnvəˌlop]	信封

track 48

4.10

剪頭髮

會話實例

Ⓐ Hi! I'd like to have a haircut.

我想要剪頭髮。

Ⓑ Sure, have a seat. Would you like any drinks?

好的,請坐。你要喝點什麼嗎?

A Green tea, please.

麻煩給我綠茶。

B Do you have anything particular in mind?

你有特別想要剪怎樣嗎？

A Nothing specific. But I want something different this time.

沒有特別的想法，但我這次想換換髮型。

B How about we make it shorter, with bangs?

我們這次剪短一點如何，剪劉海？

A Ok, can you also layer it?

好呀，你可以打層次嗎？

B Sure.

當然。

延伸例句

▶ I'd like to book a haircut.
我想要預約剪髮。

▶ I'd like to get a haircut.
我想要剪頭髮。

▶ I got a haircut.
我剪頭髮了。

▶ You look sharp with the new haircut.
你新髮型很帥。

4 當地生活篇

▷ Did you have your hair cut?
你剪頭髮了嗎？

▷ My hair needs trimming.
我頭髮該修一修。

▷ Just give the ends a trim, please.
請把髮尾修一修就行。

▷ I went to the hairdressers for a shampoo and set.
我去美髮店洗頭還有做頭髮。

▷ How much do you charge for a shampoo?
請問洗髮收費多少錢？

▷ I'd like to get my hair straightened.
我想把頭髮燙直。

▷ I'd like some gold highlights.
我要挑染金色。

▷ I'd like to have the style like in this picture.
我想剪成像這張照片的髮型。

▷ I usually don't spend much time on my hair.
我通常不會花很多時間弄頭髮。

▷ I'd like to get a perm to give my hair more volume.
我想燙頭髮，讓我的頭髮更豐盈。

▶ Do you have any suggestions?
你有建議嗎？

▶ I'd like to dye my hair black.
我想要把頭髮染黑。

▶ I want a lighter hair color.
我想要更淺的髮色。

▶ I'd like to have a high fade on the sides.
我想要兩邊高一點的剷青。

▶ My hair is a bit wavy.
我的頭髮有點捲。

▶ I'd like to have a low-maintenance and easy haircut.
我想要一個好整理、簡單的髮型。

▶ I'd like to keep my curly hair short and easy to maintain.
我想要剪短我的捲髮，比較好整理。

▶ Do you sell dandruff shampoos?
你們有賣頭皮屑專用洗髮精嗎？

4 當地生活篇

相關單字、片語

haircut [ˈhɛr͵kʌt]	理髮	
particular [pəˈtɪkjələ]	特殊的；特定的；特別的	
specific [sprˈsɪfɪk]	特殊的，特定的	

bang [bæŋ]	前劉海
layer [`leɚ]	把…修剪出層次
sharp [ʃɑrp]	時髦的，漂亮的
hair [hɛr]	毛髮；頭髮
trim [trɪm]	修剪；修整
end [ɛnd]	末端；盡頭
hairdresser [`hɛrˌdrɛsɚ]	美髮師
shampoo [ʃæm`pu]	洗髮；洗頭
set [sɛt]	使（頭髮）成型
straighten [`stretn]	把……弄直
highlight [`haɪˌlaɪt]	突出加亮
usually [`juʒʊəlɪ]	通常地；慣常地
perm [pɝm]	燙髮
volume [`vɑljəm]	體積；容積
suggestion [sə`dʒɛstʃən]	建議，提議
light [laɪt]	明亮的；淺色的
fade [fed]	褪色，消失
wavy [`wevɪ]	呈波浪形的；稍稍捲曲的
low [lo]	少的，小的，低的
maintenance [`mentənəns]	維持，保持
curly [`kɝlɪ]	有鬈髮的
maintain [men`ten]	維持；保持
dandruff [`dændrəf]	頭皮屑

○track 49

4.11 美容院

會話實例

🅐 I'd like to get a manicure today.
我今天想要做指甲。

🅑 How would you like your nails painted today?
你今天指甲想要做怎樣？

🅐 I want to do gel nails.
我想要做光療。

🅑 Sure. Here are the colors for you to choose.
好的，這邊是你可以選擇的顏色。

🅐 How much does the gel manicure cost?
做光療要多少錢？

🅑 The classic gel manicure treatment will be 130 AED. We have a promotion today, 150 AED for manicure plus pedicure.
經典光療療程是130阿聯酋迪拉姆，我們今天有促銷活動，手加腳的美甲只要150阿聯酋迪拉姆。

A Hmmm...Ok, I'll take that. Can I also have eyebrow threading?

嗯...好的,那我做這個。我能順便做眉毛除毛嗎?

B Sure. Please have a seat here.

當然,這邊請坐。

延伸例句

▶ I am going to the beauty salon to get a manicure and a pedicure.

我要去美容院做手腳的指甲。

▶ Where did you have your gel nails done?

你的光療指甲是去哪裡做的?

▶ I'd like to get a chin and upper lip threading.

我想要做下巴及嘴唇上方的除毛。

▶ I got my eyebrows threaded.

我去挽眉了。

▶ I had a full face threading, it was painful!

我做了全臉挽面,好痛!

▶ That manicurist is very good at nail art.

那位美甲師做的彩繪指甲很棒。

▶ It took me two hours for my gel nail treatment.

我做光療指甲花了兩小時。

▶ Gel nail polish lasts longer than the regular nail polish.

凝膠指甲油比一般指甲油維持的久。

▶ Can you please trim my eyebrows?

你可以幫我修眉毛嗎？

▶ I'd like to remove the gel nails.

我想要卸除凝膠指甲。

▶ I'd like to do French manicure.

我想要做法式指甲。

▶ I'm thinking about getting eyelash extensions.

我正在考慮要去接睫毛。

▶ I'd like to do facial waxing.

我想做臉部熱蠟除毛。

▶ I'd like to do full legs hair removal.

我想做全腿除毛。

▶ How much does a full back waxing cost?

全背除毛要多少錢？

4 當地生活篇

相關單字、片語

manicure [ˋmænɪˌkjʊr]	修指甲
nail[nel]	（手，腳的）指甲
paint [pent]	油漆；塗以顏色
gel [dʒɛl]	膠體；凝膠

choose [tʃuz]	選擇；挑選
treatment [`tritmənt]	治療
pedicure [`pɛdɪˌkjʊr]	足部治療；修趾甲術
eyebrow [`aɪˌbraʊ]	眉，眉毛
threading [`θrɛd.ɪŋ]	（用長細線給面部）除毛
beauty [`bjutɪ]	美，美麗，優美
salon [sə`lɑn]	（營業性的）廳，院，室，店
chin [tʃɪn]	頦，下巴
upper [`ʌpɚ]	上面的
lip [lɪp]	嘴唇
thread [θrɛd]	使交織；穿（針，線等）；通，通過；穿過
face [fes]	臉，面孔
painful [`penfəl]	疼痛的；引起痛苦的
manicurist [`mænɪˌkjʊrɪst]	指甲修飾師
nail polish	指甲油
polish [`pɑlɪʃ]	磨光粉；擦亮劑
remove [rɪ`muv]	脫掉；去掉，消除
French [frɛntʃ]	法國的；法語的
eyelash [`aɪˌlæʃ]	（一根）睫毛
extension [ɪk`stɛnʃən]	伸展；延長
facial [`feʃəl]	臉的；面部的
wax [wæks]	給……上蠟
leg [lɛg]	腿，足；小腿
removal [rɪ`muv!]	除去；削除；排除
back [bæk]	背脊，背部

4.12 去按摩

會話實例

Ⓐ Hello, how may I help you?

您好，需要什麼服務嗎？

Ⓑ I'd like to make a reservation for a massage at 15:00.

我想要預約下午三點的按摩。

Ⓐ Ok. Which type of massage would you like to have?

好的，你想要哪種按摩服務？

Ⓑ How much is it for a 2 hours full body oil massage?

請問兩小時全身精油按摩怎麼收費？

Ⓐ That'll be 70 EUR.

70歐元。

Ⓑ What about 90 minutes?

那90分鐘呢？

Ⓐ 50 EUR.

50歐元。

❹ 當地生活篇

B I'll have a 90 minutes massage, please. Thank you.

我選 90 分鐘的按摩,謝謝。

延伸例句

▶ I'd like to have a foot massage.
我想要做腳底按摩。

▶ I'd like to have a deep tissue massage.
我想要做深層組織按摩。

▶ I'd like a female therapist, please.
我想要女性按摩師。

▶ Do you have therapeutic massage?
你們有提供治療按摩嗎?

▶ I'd like to have a body scrub.
我要做全身去角質。

▶ Do you offer hot stone massage?
你們有提供熱石按摩嗎?

▶ What packages do you have?
你們有什麼包套服務嗎?

▶ How long is a full body massage?
全身按摩要多久時間?

▶ I have stiff neck.
我的脖子很僵硬。

▶ Would you massage my shoulders?
你可以幫我按摩肩膀嗎？

▶ How is the pressure?
力道還好嗎？

▶ A bit softer, please.
請按輕一點。

▶ Harder, please.
請按大力一點。

▶ I'm feeling ticklish, could you avoid this spot, please?
我覺得很癢，可以麻煩你避開這個點嗎？

▶ I'm feeling cold, can I please have an electric blanket?
我覺得很冷，可以麻煩你給我電熱毯嗎？

❹ 當地生活篇

相關單字、片語

reservation [ˌrɛzəˋveʃən] 預訂；預訂的房間	
body [ˋbɑdɪ]	身體；肉體
oil [ɔɪl]	油
massage [məˋsɑʒ]	n. 按摩 v. 給……按摩（或推拿）
foot [fʊt]	腳，足
deep [dip]	深的；位於深處的
tissue [ˋtɪʃʊ]	組織

female [ˋfimel]	女（性）的
therapist [ˋθɛrəpɪst]	治療學家；特定療法技師（或專家）
therapeutic [ˌθɛrəˋpjutɪk]	治療的；治療學的；有療效的
scrub [skrʌb]	擦洗，擦
stone [ston]	石，石頭，石塊
package [ˋpækɪdʒ]	有關聯的）一組事物，一攬子交易（計畫，建議等）
stiff [stɪf]	僵直的，僵硬的
neck [nɛk]	頸，脖子
shoulder [ˋʃoldɚ]	肩，肩膀
pressure [ˋprɛʃɚ]	治療的；有療效的
soft [sɔft]	低的，輕柔的；虛弱的，軟弱的
hard [hard]	猛力的；辛苦的
ticklish [ˋtɪk!ɪʃ]	易癢的；怕癢的
spot [spat]	場所，地點
electric blanket	電毯
electric [ɪˋlɛktrɪk]	電的；導電的
blanket [ˋblæŋkɪt]	毛毯，毯子

去圖書館

會話實例

Ⓐ Hello, I'd like to check out these books.
哈囉，我想要借這些書。

Ⓑ Sure, may I have your library card?
好的，可以給我你的借閱證嗎？

Ⓐ Here. How long can I check out these books?
給你，這些書可以借多久？

Ⓑ They may be checked out for up to 20 days.
這些書可以借20天。

Ⓐ Can I renew them?
我可以續借嗎？

Ⓑ They may be renewed twice for three weeks each, as long as no one else is waiting for the books.
只要沒有其他人在等待這些書，可以續借兩次，一次各是三禮拜。

❹ 當地生活篇

A That's great! Thank you.

太好了！謝謝你。

B Enjoy reading!

閱讀愉快！

延伸例句

▷ I'd like to apply for a library card.

我想要申請借閱證。

▷ What time do you open?

你們幾點開？

▷ What are your hours of operation?

你們的營業時間是幾點？

▷ How late are you open till tonight?

你們今晚開到幾點？

▷ The library is closed for cleaning and maintenance.

圖書館閉館清潔維修。

▷ Can I print in the library?

我能在圖書館印東西嗎？

▷ Do the libraries offer photocopying and scanning service?

圖書館有提供影印及掃瞄服務嗎？

▶ What's the fine for overdue books?
逾期未還的書罰款是多少？

▶ I borrowed these novels from the public library.
我從公共圖書館借了這些小說。

▶ The library is giving away old magazines for free.
圖書館在贈送舊雜誌。

▶ What's the maximum number of times I can renew the book?
這本書最多可以續借幾次？

▶ How long can reference materials be checked out?
參考資料可以借閱多久？

▶ These books may be checked out for up to 3 weeks.
這些書可以被借出三禮拜。

---

❹ 當地生活篇

▶ I'm looking for the reference shelves, can you please point them out to me?
我正在找參考書架，你可以指給我看它們在哪嗎？

▶ I'm looking for this book, can you help me with it?
我正在找這本書，可以麻煩你幫我嗎？

► How many books can I check out?
我可以借閱多少本書？

► How to use the self-checkout machines?
要如何使用自動借閱機？

► Can I return books to any locations?
我可以在任何其他地點還書嗎？

► Where can I find the library webinars schedule?
我要在哪裡可以找到圖書館線上研討會時間表？

► I made a request for a book.
我申請預訂了一本書。

► I'd like to pick up the book I requested.
我想要領取我預定的書。

► Do you have study rooms?
你們有讀書室嗎？

► Where can I find a computer?
哪裡有電腦？

► How do I read a book online?
我要如何在線上看書？

► Do you have children's books?
你們有童書嗎？

► How do I donate books to the library?
要如何捐贈書給圖書館？

▶ You can ask the librarians at the circulation desk.
你可以去還書處問圖書館員。

相關單字、片語

library [ˈlaɪˌbrɛrɪ]	圖書館，藏書室
renew [rɪˈnju]	續借；續訂
twice [twaɪs]	兩次，兩回
wait [wet]	等，等待
read [rid]	讀，閱讀
operation [ˌɑpəˈreʃən]	經營；營運
hour [aʊr]	小時；時刻
tonight [təˈnaɪt]	在今晚
cleaning [ˈklinɪŋ]	打掃；去汙
print [prɪnt]	印，印刷
photocopying [ˈfəʊtəʊˌkɒpiːɪŋ]	複印
scanning [ˈskænɪŋ]	電子光束掃掠
overdue [ˈovəˈdju]	過期的；未兌的
novel [ˈnɑvl̩]	（長篇）小說
give away	贈送；分發
magazine [ˌmægəˈzin]	雜誌，期刊
material [məˈtɪrɪəl]	素材；資料
shelf [ʃɛlf]	（書櫥等的）架子
point out	指出，提出
webinar [ˈwebɪnɑː(r)]	網路研討會
request [rɪˈkwɛst]	要求，請求；請求的事

❹ 當地生活篇

children [ˈtʃɪldrən]	child的名詞複數，小孩，兒童
donate [ˈdonet]	捐獻，捐贈
librarian [laɪˈbrɛrɪən]	圖書館員
circulation [ˌsɝkjəˈleʃən]	流通，傳播
desk [dɛsk]	書桌；櫃臺；服務臺

5

飲食篇

5.1 餐廳訂位

會話實例

A Danny's Steakhouse. What may I assist you?

丹尼牛排館,可以為您服務嗎?

B I'd like to make a reservation.

我想要訂位。

A Sure. Which day and at what time?

好的,哪天以及哪個時段呢?

B This saturday night, at 7pm.

這個星期六晚上七點。

A Certainly. For how many people?

好的,幾位呢?

B 7 adults and one infant.

七個大人和一個嬰兒。

A Sure, we'll prepare a baby high chair for you. Would you like to sit indoors or outdoors?

好的,我們會準備嬰兒高腳椅給您,想要坐室內還是室外呢?

5 飲食篇

B Indoors, please.
室內。

延伸例句

▶ I'd like to make a reservation for 2.
我想要訂位，有兩人。

▶ I'd like to reserve a table for 4 people, today at 7pm.
我想要訂四人位，今天晚上七點。

▶ Can I make a reservation for tonight?
今天晚上還有位子嗎？

▶ Can you reserve tables for 12 people?
我可以保留十二人的座位嗎？

▶ Can I book a section of the restaurant for a birthday party?
我可以預訂餐廳的其中一區來舉辦慶生派對嗎？

▶ May I know your last name, please?
請問您姓什麼？

▶ May I have your phone number?
請給我您的手機號碼。

▶ When is your reservation for?
您要訂什麼時候呢？

▶ It's for tomorrow evening at 6.
明天晚上六點。

▶ For how many people?
幾位呢？

▶ When is it for?
什麼時間呢？

▶ For what time?
什麼時間呢？

▶ Would you prefer a smoking or non-smoking area?
請問要在吸菸區還是禁菸區呢？

▶ I'd like a table in the non-smoking area.
我想要禁菸區的座位。

▶ Would you likc a corner table or a middle table?
您想要靠角落還是中間的座位？

▶ Can I have a table next to the window?
我可以選靠窗的座位嗎？

▶ Would you like to pick another time?
您想要選別的時段嗎？

▶ It's fully booked for this weekend.
這週末的位子都滿了。

▶ Sorry. The reservations for today are full.
很抱歉，今天的訂位都滿了。

- ▶ We are fully booked at the moment, would you like to arrange another time?
  我們這個時間已經訂滿了，請問要改別的時間嗎？

- ▶ Would you like to come in earlier?
  您想要早一點來嗎？

- ▶ Ok. We have reserved your table for 4.
  好的，我們已經為您保留四人訂位。

- ▶ Your reservation has been confirmed. Thanks for calling.
  您的預訂已完成，感謝您的來電。

- ▶ How long will you hold my reservation?
  我的訂位您會保留多久呢？

- ▶ We'll hold your table for 15 minutes.
  我們會為您保留座位十五分鐘。

- ▶ I'd like to cancel the reservation I made for this Friday under the name of Hsu.
  我想取消這禮拜五的訂位，我姓許。

相關單字、片語

night [naɪt]	夜；晚上
people [ˋpip!]	人們
adult [əˋdʌlt]	成年的；成年人的
baby [ˋbebɪ]	嬰兒的

chair [tʃɛr]	椅子
outdoors [ˈaʊtˈdorz]	在戶外，在野外
reserve [rɪˈzɝv]	保留；預約，預訂
section [ˈsɛkʃən]	（事物的）部分
restaurant [ˈrɛstərənt]	餐廳，餐館
party [ˈpɑrtɪ]	聚會，集會，派對
know [no]	知道；了解
phone [fon]	電話
evening [ˈivnɪŋ]	傍晚；晚上
prefer [prɪˈfɝ]	更喜歡
smoking [ˈsmokɪŋ]	抽菸，吸菸
corner [ˈkɔrnə]	在角落的
middle [ˈmɪdl̩]	中部的，中間的
view [vju]	景色
pick [pɪk]	挑選，選擇
weekend [ˈwikˌɛnd]	週末；週末的休假
earlier [ˈɝlɪr]	早先的時候
confirm [kənˈfɝm]	證實；確定
hold [hold]	持續，保持
under [ˈʌndə]	（表從屬）在……的管理（或統治、領導、監督）之下

track 53

5.2
餐廳帶位

會話實例

A Good evening. Do you have a reservation?
晚上好，您有預約訂位嗎？

B No, may I have a table for 5, please?
沒有，可以給我五人座嗎？

A One moment, please.
請稍候。

B Sure, thank you.
好的，謝謝你。

A Thank you for waiting. Your table is ready. Please follow me.
謝謝您們的等待，您們的餐桌已準備好，請跟我來。

B Great! Thank you!
太好了！謝謝你！

A Can I start you off with anything to drink?
您們想要先喝點什麼嗎？

B Yes, can I have a glass of lemonade?
要，可以給我一杯檸檬水嗎？

延伸例句

▶ How many people?
有幾位？

▶ There are two of us.
兩位。

▶ I have a reservation for Johnson.
我有訂位，訂位姓名是強生。

▶ I have a reservation under the name of Marlin.
我有預約，訂位姓名是馬林。

▶ I booked a table for 2 at 8pm.
我訂了八點兩位。

▶ May I have a table for 4?
可以請你給我四人位嗎？

▶ We're a bit busy right now. Would you like to wait for 20 minutes?
現在餐廳人很多，請問您願意等待20分鐘嗎？

▶ It will be a few minutes.
請稍等幾分鐘。

▶ I'll show you to your table now.
我帶您到您的座位。

▶ Please follow me.
請跟我來。

⑤
飲食篇

▶ Come this way, please.
這邊請。

▶ Your table isn't quite ready yet.
您的位子還沒準備好。

▶ Would you like to wait in the bar?
您想在酒吧等候嗎？

▶ Could you tell me where the restroom is?
請問廁所在哪裡？

▶ Do you need a few more minutes?
您還需要幾分鐘嗎？

▶ Let me know when you're ready to order.
等您們準備好要點餐時跟我說。

▶ Are you ready to order?
您準備好要點餐了嗎？

▶ May I take your order?
我能為您點餐嗎？

▶ We're ready to order.
我們準備好要點餐了。

▶ We'd like a little longer, please.
我們還需要一點時間。

相關單字、片語

lemonade [ˌlɛmən`ed]	檸檬水
busy [`bɪzɪ]	忙碌的，繁忙的
way [we]	方向
ready [`rɛdɪ]	準備好的
yet [jɛt]	還（沒）
bar [bɑr]	酒吧
restroom ['restruːm]	洗手間
long [lɔŋ]	長的；遠的；長久的

 track 54

5.3
餐廳點餐

會話實例

A Here is the menu. Can I get you anything to drink?
這是菜單，請問您要喝點什麼嗎？

B We'd like some sparkling wine, please.
我們想點氣泡酒。

A Excellent, I'll be right back.
好的，我馬上回來。

飲食篇

A Are you ready to order?

您準備好要點餐了嗎？

B Yes, I'd like smoked salmon crostini for starter, and lobster for main course.

好了，我想要煙燻鮭魚脆餅當開胃菜，龍蝦當主菜。

C I'd like chicken salad and grilled tuna with asparagus.

我想要雞肉沙拉和烤鮪魚佐蘆筍。

A Can I get you anything else?

還需要什麼嗎？

C No, thank you.

不用，謝謝。

延伸例句

▶ Any questions about the menu?

對菜單有任何疑問嗎？

▶ Do you have any vegetarian dishes?

你們有任何素食餐點嗎？

▶ What are the vegetarian options?

有什麼素食的選擇？

▶ Is this served with salad?

這有附沙拉嗎？

▶ That comes with a baked potato and a salad.

副餐有烤馬鈴薯和沙拉。

▶ Can I see the wine list, please?
可以給我看酒單嗎？

▶ What's on the menu today?
今天菜單上有什麼菜？

▶ What's today's special?
今日特餐是什麼？

▶ What do you recommend?
你有什麼建議嗎？

▶ I recommand the lobster roll as starter.
我推薦龍蝦捲當前菜。

▶ The chef's special is very popular.
主廚特選很受歡迎。

▶ Would you care for an appetizer?
您想要開胃菜嗎？

▶ Anything to drink?
您要喝飲料嗎？

▶ Just water for me.
我喝水就好。

▶ Would you like a starter?
您想要前菜嗎？

▶ For starter, I'd like some leek soup.
我想要韭蔥湯作為前菜。

▶ I'll have the rib-eye steak.
我想要肋眼牛排。

▶ How would you like that cooked?
您想要幾分熟？

▶ Medium, please.
五分熟。

▶ Medium rare, please.
三分熟。

▶ How do you like your steak?
牛排要幾分熟？

▶ I'd like my steak well done.
我的牛排要九分熟。

▶ How do you like your eggs done?
您的蛋想要用什麼方式料理呢？

▶ Soft boiled, please.
半熟水煮蛋。

▶ What kind of dressing would you like on your salad?
您要哪種沙拉醬料呢？

▶ What dressings do you have?
你們有哪些沙拉醬呢？

▶ Can I have the dressing on the side?
可以把我的沙拉醬放在旁邊嗎？

▶ Would you like anything else?
　您還要點其他東西嗎？

▶ That'll be fine for now, thank you.
　目前先這樣就好，謝謝。

▶ Will that be all?
　全部就這樣嗎？

▶ Yes, that's it.
　是的，就這樣。

▶ Your order is coming right up.
　您點的餐很快就來了。

▶ Your main dish will be out soon.
　即將為您上主餐。

▶ Enjoy your meal!
　用餐愉快！

▶ Could we have 2 more forks, please?
　可以再給我們兩隻叉子嗎？

▶ Excuse me, this isn't what I ordered.
　不好意思，這不是我點的餐。

▶ Oh, I'm so sorry. I'll change it for you
　straightaway.
　噢，我很抱歉，我馬上為您換餐。

▶ This is too salty!
　這太鹹了！

▶ This is cold.
這冷掉了。

▶ Did you enjoy your meal?
您喜歡您的餐點嗎？

▶ Would you like something for dessert?
您要甜點嗎？

▶ I'll have chocolate mousse cake, please.
我要巧克力慕斯蛋糕。

▶ Any coffee or tea with your dessert?
需要咖啡或茶搭配您的甜點嗎？

▶ No, I think I'm good. Thank you.
不用，謝謝。

▶ Are there any nuts in it? I'm allergic to nuts.
裡面有任何堅果嗎？我對堅果過敏。

相關單字、片語

drink [drɪŋk]	飲，喝
sparkling [ˋspɑrklɪŋ]	起泡沫的
wine [waɪn]	葡萄酒；水果酒
smoked [smokt]	燻製的；用煙處理的
salmon [ˋsæmən]	鮭魚
starter [ˋstɑrtɚ]	開胃菜；第一道菜
lobster [ˋlɑbstɚ]	大螯蝦；龍蝦

main [men]	主要的，最重要的
course [kors]	一道菜
salad [`sæləd]	沙拉
grilled [grɪld]	烤的；炙過的
asparagus [ə`spærəgəs]	蘆筍
question [`kwɛstʃən]	問題；詢問
bake [bek]	烘，烤
potato [pə`teto]	馬鈴薯；洋芋
list [lɪst]	表；名冊；目錄
recommend [ˌrɛkə`mɛnd]	推薦，介紹
roll [rol]	麵包捲；捲餅
popular [`pɑpjələ]	受歡迎的
appetizer [`æpəˌtaɪzə]	開胃的食物
leek [lik]	韭蔥
steak [stek]	牛排
medium [`midɪəm]	（肉）燒得適中的，中等熟度的
boiled [bɔɪld]	煮沸的；煮熟的
dressing [`drɛsɪŋ]	（拌沙拉等用的）調料
meal [mil]	膳食；一餐
fork [fɔrk]	叉
straightaway [`stretəˌwe]	儘快地；立刻
salty [`sɔltɪ]	有鹽分的
mousse [mus]	（多泡沫的）奶油甜點

5.4 餐廳結帳

會話實例

A How was your meal?
您的餐點如何?

B It was very delicious.
很好吃。

A Can I get you anything else?
您還需要什麼嗎?

B Could I have a to go container for this?
可以給我一個外帶餐盒嗎?

A Of course. One moment, please.
當然,請稍候。

C Could we also have the check, please?
可以順便給我們帳單嗎?

A Certainly. How would you like to pay?
好的,您想要如何付款?

B By credit card.
信用卡。

延伸例句

▶ Was everything alright?
一切都好嗎？

▶ Did you enjoy your meal?
您喜歡您的餐點嗎？

▶ Thank you for your feedback.
謝謝您的意見回饋。

▶ Could we have the bill?
可以給我們帳單嗎？

▶ I'd like the check, pleasc.
請給我帳單。

▶ Separate checks, pleaese.
我們要分開帳單。

▶ Let's share the bill.
我們一起付吧。

▶ I'll get this.
我來付吧。

▶ Keep the change.
不用找了。

▶ Thank you for your service!
謝謝您的服務！

▶ See you next time!
下次見！

▶ Hope to see you soon!
希望很快再見到您！

▶ Thank you for coming!
謝謝您們光臨！

相關單字、片語

container [kənˋtenɚ]	容器（如箱、盒、罐等）
feedback [ˋfidˏbæk]	回饋；反饋
separate [ˋsɛpəˏret]	分開的；單獨的
share [ʃɛr]	分享；分擔

track 56

速食店

會話實例

A Hi. May I take your order?
嗨，我可以幫您點餐嗎？

B I'd like a chicken burger with fries.
我想要雞肉漢堡和薯條。

Ⓐ Would you like anything to drink?
你要飲料嗎？

Ⓑ Sprite, please.
請給我雪碧。

Ⓐ It's for here or to go?
內用還是外帶？

Ⓑ For here, please.
這邊用。

Ⓐ It's 7 dollars.
這樣總共七塊錢。

Ⓑ Here you go.
給你。

延伸例句

▶ I'll have a double cheeseburger and a coke,
please.
我想要雙層起司漢堡和一杯可樂。

▶ I'll have fish burger and the combo.
我要魚肉漢堡套餐。

▶ Could I have a small pepperoni pizza?
可以給我一個小的臘腸披薩嗎？

▶ Could I get a shawarma and a fried chicken
combo?
可以給我一個沙威瑪跟一個炸雞套餐嗎？

Ⓢ
飲食篇

▶ Could I get 8 donuts?
可以給我八個甜甜圈嗎？

▶ Could I make that a combo?
我可以點套餐嗎？

▶ Would you like cookies or chips?
您想要餅乾還是薯片？

▶ Would you like cheese with that?
您要搭配起司嗎？

▶ Is that all you'll be ordering?
您點的全部就這樣嗎？

▶ Anything else?
還要什麼嗎？

▶ That's everything for today?
今天全部就這樣嗎？

▶ I'd like some lentil soup, too.
我也想要點扁豆湯。

▶ Is that it?
全部就這樣嗎？

▶ Yes, that's it.
是的，全部就這樣。

▶ Can I have your name for the order?
可以給我您的訂餐名字嗎？

▶ Is it for takeout?
　您是要外帶嗎？

▶ That'll be 12 dollars.
　這樣是十二元。

▶ Would you like a receipt?
　您要收據嗎？

▶ It'll take about 10 minutes.
　大概要等十分鐘。

▶ Here is your order.
　這是您的餐點。

▶ The straws are over there.
　吸管在那邊。

相關單字、片語

burger [ˈbɝgɚ]	【口】漢堡，漢堡牛肉餅
double [ˈdʌbl̩]	兩倍的；加倍的
fish [fɪʃ]	魚
combo [ˈkɑmbo]	結合（物）
pepperoni [ˌpɛpəˈronɪ]	義大利辣味香腸
shawarma [ʃəˈwɑmə]	（阿拉伯）沙威瑪烤肉
fried [fraɪd]	油炸的
donut [ˈdoˌnʌt]	油炸圈餅；炸麵圈
cookie [ˈkʊki]	甜餅乾
chip [tʃɪp]	炸馬鈴薯條；炸洋芋片

⑤ 飲食篇

cheese [tʃiz]	乳酪，乾酪，起司
lentil [ˋlɛntɪl]	濱豆，扁豆
takeout [ˋtekˏaʊt]	帶出去，取出；外賣
straw [strɔ]	吸管

track 57

5.6 咖啡店

會話實例

🅐 Coffee House, what can I get you today?

咖啡家，您今天想點什麼？

🅑 Could I please get a large cappuccino?

可以給我一杯大杯卡布奇諾嗎？

🅐 Any sugar?

要加糖嗎？

🅑 No, thank you.

不用，謝謝。

🅐 Would you like to try our new chestnut cake?

您要試試看我們新出的栗子蛋糕嗎？

🅑 Okay, I'll get that.

好呀，我點一份。

A Your total is \$11.

總共十一元。

B Here.

這邊。

延伸例句

▶ Can I have 2 iced lattes, please?

請給我兩杯冰美式。

▶ One double espresso, one Americano, please.

一杯濃縮咖啡、一杯美式。

▶ Can I get a decaf coffee, please?

可以給我一杯低咖啡因咖啡嗎？

▶ Can I have cream and caramel in it, please?

我可以加奶油跟焦糖嗎？

▶ I'd like a latte with oat milk.

我想要燕麥奶拿鐵。

▶ I'd like a strawberry waffle.

我想要一份草莓鬆餅。

▶ I'll have black tea chiffon cake.

我要紅茶戚風蛋糕。

▶ Can I have almond milk instead of cow milk?

我可以用杏仁奶取代牛奶嗎？

5 飲食篇

▶ Do you have coconut milk?
你們有椰奶嗎?

相關單字、片語

house [haʊs]	房子;住宅
cappuccino [ˌkɑpəˋtʃino]	卡布奇諾咖啡
sugar [ˋʃʊgɚ]	糖
chestnut [ˋtʃɛsˌnʌt]	栗子
total [ˋtotl]	總數;合計
iced [aɪst]	冰過的;冰鎮的
espresso [ɛsˋprɛso]	用蒸汽加壓煮出的)濃咖啡
decaf = decaffeinated [diˋkæfɪˌnetɪd]	
	脫除咖啡因的
cream [krim]	奶油;乳脂
caramel [ˋkærəml]	焦糖
oat [ot]	燕麥
strawberry [ˋstrɔbɛrɪ]	草莓
chiffon [ʃɪˋfɑn]	鬆軟的
waffle [ˋwɑfl]	鬆餅
almond [ˋɑmənd]	杏仁
instead [ɪnˋstɛd]	作為替代
coconut [ˋkəʊkənʌt]	椰子

5.7 叫外賣

會話實例

A Hello. Nora's Thai food.
哈囉，諾拉泰式料理。

B I'd like to order, please.
我想要點餐。

A Pick-up or delivery?
現場取餐還是外送。

B Delivery.
外送。

A Alright. What's your address and phone number?
好的，您的地址及電話？

B 35 Pine Street, Apartment 7. My phone number is 04-2665200.
松樹街35號，7號房。我的電話號碼是04-2665200。

A What would you like to order?
你要點什麼？

B One pad Thai, and 4 shrimp spring rolls.
一個泰式米粉、四個蝦肉春捲。

5 飲食篇

延伸例句

▶ How much will that be?
總共多少錢?

▶ How are you paying?
請問您的付款方式?

▶ Would you like cutleries?
你需要餐具嗎?

▶ Anything else?
還有需要什麼嗎?

▶ Could you please send some chili sauce?
可以麻煩你給我辣椒醬嗎?

▶ Could I have extra plates, please?
可以給我多的盤子嗎?

▶ How much is the delivery fee?
外送費是多少?

▶ If your order is more than 50 dollars, we'll waive your delivery fee.
如果您的訂購金額超過五十元,我們將免除運費。

▶ How long will it take?
會花多久時間?

▶ About 30 minutes.
大概三十分鐘。

▶ It'll take approximately 40 minutes.
　大約四十分鐘。

▶ Your order will arrive in an hour.
　您的餐點將在一小時內送達。

▶ I haven't received my order yet.
　我還沒收到我的餐點。

相關單字、片語

pine [paɪn]	松樹
shrimp [ʃrɪmp]	（小）蝦
spring [sprɪŋ]	春季，春天
cutlery [ˋkʌtlərɪ]	餐具
send [sɛnd]	發送，寄
chili [ˋtʃɪlɪ]	紅番椒
sauce [sɔs]	調味醬，醬汁
plate [plet]	盤子，盆
waive [wev]	放棄；免除
approximately [əˋprɑksəmɪtlɪ]	大概；近乎
receive [rɪˋsiv]	收到，接到

6

購物篇

6.1

逛超市

會話實例

A Excuse me, I'm looking for tomatoes.

不好意思,我在找番茄。

B Oh, I'm sorry. They're sold out.

喔,很抱歉,番茄賣完了。

A I see. Thank you.

好的,謝謝。

B If you don't mind using a substitute, we have canned tomato sauce.

如果你不介意使用替代品,我們有罐裝蕃茄糊。

A Yea! Can you please tell me where it is?

好呀!麻煩你告訴我在哪。

B Sure, it's in the third aisle from the entrance.

好的,從入口數來第三排。

A Thank you very much for your help.

感謝你的幫忙。

B You're welcome.

不客氣。

延伸例句

▶ I need to pick up a few things in the supermarket.
我需要去超市買幾樣東西。

▶ I want to do grocery shopping.
我想去採買東西。

▶ I'll get a shopping cart.
我去拿購物推車。

▶ Where do I find the mayonnaise?
美乃滋在哪裡？

▶ Is it organic?
這是有機的嗎？

▶ Where can I find fish sauce?
請問魚露在哪裡？

▶ I'm looking for condensed milk.
我在找煉乳。

▶ I'm after cheese, can you show me where it is?
我在找起司，可以請你告訴我在哪嗎？

▶ The potatoes are in the produce section.
馬鈴薯在農產品區。

▶ The milk is in aisle 7.
牛奶在第七排。

▶ It's down the aisle.
在這排最後面。

▶ Do you sell tahini?
你們有賣芝麻醬嗎？

▶ Sorry, we don't carry this item.
抱歉，我們沒有賣這個東西。

▶ Sorry, it's sold out.
抱歉，這個賣光了。

▶ The toilet paper rolls are sold out.
捲筒衛生紙賣光了。

▶ Can I have a handful of pistachio?
我要買一把開心果。

▶ Can I have a little bit more?
麻煩再給我多一點。

▶ That's enough, thank you!
這樣就夠了，謝謝！

▶ Can I have 100g of prosciutto?
我要一百克的帕瑪火腿。

▶ I'd like some minced beef.
我要買牛絞肉。

▶ That one at the back.
後面那個。

❻ 購物篇

▶ Is this on sale?
這在特價嗎？

▶ Where is the checkout counter?
結帳櫃檯在哪裡？

▶ Are you in line?
你在排隊嗎？

▶ That comes to 136 dollars.
總共136元。

▶ Cash or credit?
付現還是刷卡？

相關單字、片語

tomato [tə`meto]	番茄
substitute [`sʌbstə,tjut]	代替人；代替物
canned [kænd]	裝成罐頭的
entrance [`ɛntrəns]	入口，門口
supermarket [`supə,mɑrkɪt]	超級市場
shopping [`ʃɑpɪŋ]	買東西，購物
grocery [`grosərɪ]	食品雜貨
cart [kɑrt]	小車，手推車
shopping cart	購物手推車
mayonnaise [,meə`nez]	蛋黃醬，美乃滋
organic [ɔr`gænɪk]	有機的
condensed [kən`dɛnst]	濃縮的

produce [prə`djus]	產品；農產品
tahini [ta`hiˌni]	芝麻糊，調味芝麻醬
toilet [`tɔɪlɪt]	廁所，洗手間
handful [`hændfəl]	一把，一握；少數，少量
pistachio [pɪs`taʃɪo]	開心果
more [mor]	更多
prosciutto [pro`ʃuto]	一種煙燻五香火腿
mince [mɪns]	切碎，剁碎
sale [sel]	賣，出；廉價出售
on sale	上市的；出售的；削價出售
checkout [`tʃɛkˌaʊt]	超級市場等的）付款臺

🎧 track 60

6.2
退換貨

會話實例

Ⓐ Hi, how may I help you?
嗨，需要什麼服務呢？

Ⓑ Hi, I'd like to return these dish drainers.
嗨，我想要退回這些碗盤濾乾架。

Ⓐ No problem. Do you have the receipts?
沒問題，您有帶發票嗎？

B Yes, here you go.

　　有，給你。

A May I also have your credit card?

　　可以也給我您的信用卡嗎？

B Yes.

　　好的。

A Great. Please sign here.

　　好的，請在這簽名。

B Sure.

　　好的。

延伸例句

▶ I'd like to get a refund.
　我想要退款。

▶ Could I please have a refund?
　我可以退款嗎？

▶ Can I ask for a refund?
　我可以要求退款嗎？

▶ Is there something wrong with it?
　有什麼問題嗎？

▶ What seems to be the problem?
　可以請問有什麼問題嗎？

► It doesn't fit.
尺寸不合。

► The trousers are too tight.
長褲太緊了。

► I bought them last week.
我上星期買的。

► Sorry, cosmetics are non-refundable.
抱歉，化妝品不可退換。

► I would like to speak to the manager.
叫你們經理出來。

► We have a special no-refund policy for underwears.
我們有一個內衣商品不退費的特別條款。

► Would you like to exchange it for something else?
您要換別的商品嗎？

► I got a refund from IKEA.
我在IKEA得到了退款。

相關單字、片語

dish [dɪʃ]	碟，盤
drainer [ˈdrenə]	濾乾器
fit [fɪt]	合身；適合

trousers [ˋtraʊzɚz]	褲子，長
tight [taɪt]	緊的
cosmetic [kɑzˋmɛtɪk]	化妝品；裝飾品
non-refundable [ˌnɑnrɪˋfʌndəbḷ]	
	不可歸還的，不可償還的
speak [spik]	說話，講話
manager [ˋmænɪdʒɚ]	負責人；主任，經理
policy [ˋpɑləsɪ]	政策，方針
underwear [ˋʌndɚˌwɛr]	內衣

track 61

6.3 買衣服

會話實例

A How may I help you?

有需要幫忙嗎？

B I'm looking for a waterproof jacket for hiking.

我在找登山用的防水外套。

A This is our most popular item.

這件是我們最受歡迎的單品。

B Can I try this on?

我能試穿這件嗎？

Ⓐ Sure, what's your size?

當然，您穿什麼尺寸呢？

Ⓑ I'll try on M.

我試穿中號的。

Ⓐ There you go. The fitting room is over there.

給您，試衣間在那邊。

Ⓑ Thank you!

謝謝！

延伸例句

▶ I'm just browsing. Thank you.
我只是看看，謝謝。

▶ I'm just looking.
我只是逛逛。

▶ I'm looking for a leather jacket.
我在找皮衣外套。

▶ Can I try this on?
我能試穿這件嗎？

▶ Do you have this in stock?
你有新的嗎？

▶ Would you like to try the coat on for size?
您想試試這件外套大小合適嗎？

▶ What is your size?
你穿幾號？

▶ What size are you?
你穿什麼尺寸？

▶ Where is the fitting room?
試衣間在哪？

▶ They're at the back.
在後面。

▶ Over there.
在那邊。

▶ How many items do you have?
你有幾件商品？

▶ Do you have this in a different color?
請問這件有別的顏色嗎？

▶ Do you have this in small?
這件有小號的嗎？

▶ Have you got it in a larger size?
有大一點的尺寸嗎？

▶ Could I have the next size up?
可以給我大一號的嗎？

▶ It's not my size.
這不是我的尺寸。

▶ It's too small.
太小了。

▶ It's too loose.
太鬆了。

▶ It doesn't fit me.
我穿不合身。

▶ I'll take it.
我要買這件。

▶ How much is this blue blouse?
這件藍色襯衫要多少錢？

▶ I can bring it to the counter for you.
我可以幫你拿去櫃台。

▶ You decided to go with the beige sweater?
您決定要一起帶這件米白毛衣嗎？

▶ I can help you at the counter.
我可以在櫃檯幫你結帳。

▶ Do you provide alteration services?
請問你們有提供修改衣服的服務嗎？

▶ How much is an alteration?
修改衣服要多少錢？

▶ Do you do alterations on jeans?
請問你們有修改牛仔褲嗎？

▶ What time do you close?
你們幾點關門？

相關單字、片語

waterproof [ˈwɔtɚ͵pruf]	不透水的，防水的
hike [haɪk]	徒步旅行，健行
fitting [ˈfɪtɪŋ]	試穿，試衣
browse [braʊz]	隨意觀看
leather [ˈlɛðɚ]	皮的；皮革製的
stock [stɑk]	進貨，庫存品，存貨
in stock	有現貨或存貨
coat [kot]	外套，大衣
loose [lus]	鬆的，寬的
blouse [blaʊz]	女裝襯衫，短上衣
decide [dɪˈsaɪd]	決定
beige [beʒ]	米色的；灰棕色的
sweater [ˈswɛtɚ]	毛線衣
alteration [͵ɔltəˈreʃən]	修改
jeans [dʒinz]	斜紋布工作褲；工裝褲，牛仔褲

6.4 買鞋子

會話實例

🅐 How may I help you?
您需要幫忙嗎？

🅑 I'm looking for shoes for walking.
我在找平時走路穿的鞋。

🅐 We have some comfortable casual shoes over here.
這邊都是一些很舒服的休閒鞋。

🅐 Can I have the black ones at the top?
我可以看最上面那雙黑色的嗎？

🅑 Sure, here they are.
當然，給您。

🅑 They look great.
看起來很棒。

🅐 Yes, would you like to try them on?
有的，您要試穿嗎？

🅑 Yeah, do you have a size 8?
好呀，你有八號嗎？

延伸例句

▶ I'm looking for a pair of sandals.
我在找一雙涼鞋。

▶ I'm looking for high heels to go with my blue dress.
我在找一雙高跟鞋來搭配我的藍色洋裝。

▶ I need new sneakers for running.
我需要跑步穿的運動鞋。

▶ What's your size?
你穿幾號的鞋？

▶ Do you have these in a 25?
這雙有沒有25號的？

▶ These are really comfortable!
這雙鞋好舒服！

▶ They are very sturdy and durable.
這雙鞋非常堅固耐用。

▶ They are made with waterproof material.
這雙鞋是防水材質。

▶ Can I try the next size down?
我可以試穿再小號一點的嗎？

▶ Do they come with another color?
這雙有別的顏色嗎？

▶ Is it on sale?
有打折嗎？

▶ I'll think about it.
我再考慮看看。

▶ Do you have shoe deodorizer?
你們有鞋子除臭劑嗎？

相關單字、片語

comfortable [ˋkʌmfɚtəb!]	使人舒服的，舒適的
casual [ˋkæʒʊəl]	不拘禮節的，非正式的
top [tɑp]	頂部
sandal [ˋsænd!]	涼鞋；拖鞋
heel [hil]	（鞋，襪等的）後跟
dress [drɛs]	洋裝
run [rʌn]	跑
sturdy [ˋstɝdɪ]	堅固的，經久耐用的
durable [ˋdjʊrəb!]	耐用的；持久的
deodorizer [diˋodəraɪzɚ]	防臭劑

🎧 track 63

6.5 買化妝品

會話實例

A Hi, are you looking for something?
嗨,您在找什麼嗎?

B I'm looking for a foundation.
我在找粉底霜。

A Have you used our products before?
您有用過我們的產品嗎?

B No. Could you please help me to choose the right color?
沒有,可以麻煩你幫我選適合的顏色嗎?

A Sure, we have a selection of 12 different colors. Would you like to try these two colors to see?
當然,這系列產品有十二種不同的顏色,您要試試看這兩個顏色嗎?

B Yea, it's just that my skin is oily, is this product good for oily skin?
好呀,但是我的皮膚是油性的,這個產品適合油性肌膚嗎?

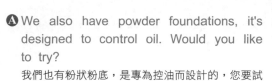
Ⓐ We also have powder foundations, it's designed to control oil. Would you like to try?

我們也有粉狀粉底,是專為控油而設計的,您要試試看嗎?

Ⓑ Yea, please.

好,麻煩你。

延伸例句

▶ What's your lipstick brand?
你的口紅是什麼牌子?

▶ Where did you buy it?
你在哪裡買的?

▶ I bought it from a local cosmetic shop.
我在當地的彩妝店買的。

▶ I like to wear make-up.
我希歡化妝。

▶ Could you show me how to use the mascara?
你可以教我塗睫毛膏嗎?

▶ What's your skin type?
你是什麼類型的肌膚?

▶ My skin is really dry.
我的皮膚很乾燥。

❻
購物篇

► It is important to moisturize before applying make-up.
  妝前保濕很重要。

► Can I apply on my face to see how it goes?
  我可以試擦在臉上看看適不適合嗎？

► Do you have any samples of this concealer?
  你們有這支遮瑕膏的試用品嗎？

► I'm looking for eyeliner.
  我在找眼線筆。

► What color do you recommend?
  你推薦什麼顏色？

► The brown eyeshadow goes well with you.
  咖啡色眼影很適合你。

► What is this cream for?
  這款乳霜的用途是什麼？

► Which of these should I apply first?
  這些我要先擦哪一個？

► You can blend all the make-up you apply with a sponge.
  你可以用海綿把化妝品暈染開。

相關單字、片語

foundation [faʊn`dcʃən]	粉底霜
selection [sə`lɛkʃən]	選擇；選拔；精選品
skin [skɪn]	皮膚，皮
oily [`ɔɪlɪ]	含）油的；多油的
powder [`paʊdɚ]	粉，粉末
design [dɪ`zaɪn]	設計；構思
control [kən`trol]	控制；支配
lipstick [`lɪpˌstɪk]	口紅
brand [brænd]	品牌；牌子
shop [ʃɑp]	商店，零售店
wear [wɛr]	穿著；戴著；佩帶著；塗抹（香水，化妝品）
mascara [mæs`kærə]	眉毛膏；睫毛膏
dry [draɪ]	乾的；乾燥的
important [ɪm`pɔrtnt]	重要的，重大的
moisturize [`mɔɪstʃəˌraɪz]	增加……的水分；使濕潤
apply [ə`plaɪ]	塗，敷；將……鋪在表面
sample [`sæmp!]	樣品，樣本；試用品
blend [blɛnd]	使混和，使混雜；使交融
sponge [spʌndʒ]	海綿

🎧 track 64

6.6 買電器用品

會話實例

Ⓐ Hello, welcome to Home Center.
哈囉，歡迎來到家庭中心。

Ⓑ Hi, how are you?
嗨，你好嗎？

Ⓐ I'm good, thank you. Do you need any help?
我很好，謝謝。你需要幫忙嗎？

Ⓑ I'm looking for an electric hair clipper.
我在找電動理髮器。

Ⓐ They're on the 3rd floor.
他們在三樓。

Ⓑ Thank you, oh, do you also have extension cords?
謝謝，噢，你們也有賣延長線嗎？

Ⓐ Yes, it's over there, please follow me.
有的，在那邊，請跟我來。

Ⓑ Thank you!
謝謝！

延伸例句

▶ I'm looking for a fan.
我在找電扇。

▶ Do you have any recommendations for vacuum machines?
你有推薦的吸塵器嗎？

▶ We need a larger TV.
我們需要更大的電視。

▶ Do you sell toasters?
你們有賣烤麵包機嗎？

▶ The refrigerators are on the second floor.
冰箱在二樓。

▶ Kitchen appliances are on the fourth floor.
廚房家電在四樓。

▶ Can I connect to this speaker and play music?
我可以連接這台音響放音樂嗎？

▶ Yes, you can connect the bluetooth speaker to your phone.
可以，你可以用手機連接藍芽音響。

▶ I'm looking for a phone charging cable.
我在尋找手機充電線。

▶ Are you offering any discount for microwaves?
　現在微波爐有打折嗎？

▶ Do you have dehumidifiers?
　你們有賣除濕機嗎？

▶ What does the warranty cover?
　請問保固服務涵蓋什麼呢？

▶ How long is the warranty?
　保固期是多久？

▶ Would you like to add a 2-Year accident protection plan on this phone?
　您想要幫手機加兩年保固方案嗎？

▶ This rice cooker is still under warranty, you could have it repaired for free.
　電鍋還在保固期內，可以免費修理。

相關單字、片語

clipper [ˈklɪpə-]	理髮剪
cord [kɔrd]	絕緣電線，軟線
fan [fæn]	扇子；風扇
vacuum [ˈvækjʊəm]	真空吸塵器
toaster [ˈtostə-]	烤麵包器
kitchen [ˈkɪtʃɪn]	廚房
appliance [əˈplaɪəns]	器具，用具；裝置
speaker [ˈspikə-]	喇叭，擴音機

cable [`keb!]	纜;索;鋼索
discount [`dɪskaʊnt]	折扣
microwave [`maɪkroˌwev]	微波爐
warranty [`wɔrəntɪ]	保證書;保單;擔保
protection [prə`tɛkʃən]	保護,防護
cooker [`kʊkə]	炊具,烹調器具
repair [rɪ`pɛr]	修理;修補

track 65

6.7

買禮物

會話實例

Ⓐ I want to buy a gift for my girlfriend. Could you help me out?

我想要幫我女朋友買禮物,你可以幫忙我嗎?

Ⓑ Sure. Do you have something in mind?

當然,你有什麼想法嗎?

Ⓐ Yes, something practical and trendy at the same time.

嗯,我想要實用又時髦的東西。

Ⓑ Well...handbags would be a good choice.

嗯...手提包應該會是個好選擇。

6 購物篇

A That's a good idea!
好主意！

B Does she have a preferred color?
她有喜歡的顏色嗎？

A Dark blue, brown, maybe beige.
深藍色、咖啡色，或許米白色。

B I'll show you our best-selling handbags.
我帶你看我們銷售最好的幾個包包。

延伸例句

▶ I want to buy my mom a birthday gift.
我想要幫我媽媽買一個生日禮物。

▶ What does she like?
她喜歡什麼呢？

▶ Do you have any suggestions?
你有任何建議嗎？

▶ What about a gift card?
買禮物卡如何？

▶ Would you wrap it as a gift?
你可以幫我包裝成禮物嗎？

▶ Could you wrap this for me?
可以麻煩你幫我包裝嗎？

► Could you gift-wrap it?
可以包裝成禮物嗎？

► We charge 2 dollars for it.
要收兩塊錢。

► Who is it for?
這是要給誰的？

► For my nephew.
是要給我的姪子。

► Could you put some ribbons on it?
你可以綁些緞帶在上面嗎？

► I bought this bag last week, but I would like to get it replaced.
我上禮拜買了這個包包，我想要退換貨。

► I would need the invoice.
我需要您的收據。

► May I ask you why you are exchanging it?
請問退換貨的理由？

相關單字、片語

gift [gɪft]	禮品
practical [`præktɪk!]	實用的
trendy [`trɛndɪ]	時髦的；流行的
handbag [`hænd͵bæg]	手提包；小旅行袋

❻ 購物篇

preferred [prɪˋfɝd]	更好的；被喜好的；優先的
best-selling [ˋbɛstˋsɛlɪŋ]	最暢銷的
nephew [ˋnɛfju]	姪兒；外甥
ribbon [ˋrɪbən]	緞帶；絲帶
replace [rɪˋples]	把……放回（原處）；取代； 以……代替

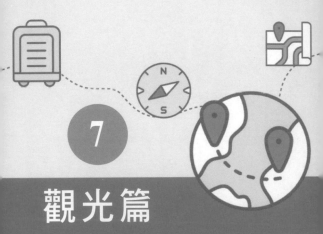

7

觀光篇

7.1 拍照

會話實例

A Excuse me, I'm traveling alone. Could you please take a photo for me?

不好意思，我一個人旅行，能麻煩你幫我拍張照嗎？

B Sure, how do I use this?

當然，這要怎麼使用？

A Just press the button on top of the camera.

按下相機上方的鈕就行了。

B Ok. I'll take a few different angles.

好的，我會幫你多拍幾張不同角度。

A Thank you so much!

太感謝你了！

B No worries! Say cheese!

不客氣！要拍了笑一個。

A Would you like me to take a photo for you, too?

你想要我幫你也拍一張嗎？

B Yea, good idea.

好呀，好主意。

延伸例句

▶ Sorry to bother you.
不好意思麻煩你。

▶ Could you take my picture please?
可以請你幫我拍張照嗎？

▶ Could you help us take a picture?
你能幫我們拍張照嗎？

▶ Could you take a picture of me with the Eiffel Tower?
你能幫我拍張跟艾非爾鐵塔的合照嗎？

▶ Would you take a picture for me and my family?
能否麻煩你幫我跟我的家人拍張照？

▶ Could you take another shot from this angle?
你可以維持這個角度幫我再拍一張嗎？

▶ Could you get the Opera House in the background?
你可以把歌劇院拍進來嗎？

▶ Can you take it in portrait (landscape) mode?
可以麻煩你拍一張直式（橫式）的照片嗎？

▶ Could you put me in the center of the picture?
可以把我放在照片中間嗎？

▶ Can I take a picture with you?
我可以跟你拍一張合照嗎？

▶ That's no problem.
沒有問題。

相關單字、片語

button [ˋbʌtn]	按鈕
picture [ˋpɪktʃɚ]	圖片；照片
angle [ˋæŋg!]	角度
family [ˋfæməlɪ]	家，家庭
shot [ʃɑt]	拍攝
background [ˋbækˌgraʊnd]	背景
portrait [ˋportret]	肖像，畫像；相片
landscape [ˋlændˌskep]	風景，景色；風景繪畫
mode [mod]	形式，型；種類
Camera lens	鏡頭

🎧 track 67

7.2 服務中心

會話實例

Ⓐ Hello, welcome to Budapest.
哈囉，歡迎來到布達佩斯。

Ⓑ Thanks. This is our first time here. We're not very familiar with the city yet.
謝謝，這是我們第一次來這裡，我們對市區還不是很熟。

Ⓐ I'd suggest you use the half-day city tour service.
我建議你可以參考半日行程的服務。

Ⓑ How much is the fee?
費用是多少？

Ⓐ It's for free.
是免費的。

Ⓑ That's great! We'll think about it!
真棒！我們考慮一下！

Ⓐ Would you like a sightseeing brochure?
你要觀光手冊嗎？

B Yes, thanks!
好呀,謝拉!

延伸例句

▶ We would like to visit the island, where can we buy the boat ticket?
我們想要參觀小島,哪裡可以買船票?

▶ We'd like to visit the winery, do we have to book it?
我們想參觀酒莊,需要先預定嗎?

▶ Can you make a reservation for us?
你可以幫我們預約嗎?

▶ I'd like to book the winery tour.
我想要訂酒莊行程。

▶ I'd like to book the walking tour in the city.
我想要預訂城市健走行程。

▶ Do you have English tours?
你們有英文行程嗎?

▶ Do you have one-day tours?
你們有一日遊行程嗎?

▶ Do you have culture tours?
你們有文化體驗行程嗎?

▶ Do you have package tours?
你們有套裝行程嗎？

▶ Can you recommend local travel agencies?
可以介紹本地的旅行社嗎？

▶ What are the cultural heritage sites here?
這裡有哪些文化古蹟？

▶ How do we go to the art museum?
美術館要怎麼去？

▶ You can take bus 10.
您可以搭乘十號巴士。

▶ You can take the tourist shuttle bus.
您可以搭乘遊客接駁車。

▶ Where's the money exchange?
外幣收兌處在哪裡？

▶ When will the theater open?
劇場幾點開門？

▶ Do you need a city map?
你需要市區地圖嗎？

▶ Can I take a metro route map?
我可以拿一張地鐵路線圖嗎？

▶ Would you like a restaurant guide?
你要餐廳指南嗎？

▶ Do you know a good place for ice cream?
  你知道哪裡有好吃的冰淇淋嗎？

▶ For authentic cuisine, I recommend "Mama's food."
  對於道地美食餐廳，我推薦「媽媽菜餚」。

相關單字、片語

familiar [fə`mɪljə]	世所周知的；熟悉的
suggest [sə`dʒɛst]	建議，提議
sightseeing [`saɪt,siɪŋ]	觀光，遊覽
brochure [bro`ʃʊr]	小冊子
island [`aɪlənd]	島；島狀物
boat [bot]	小船
winery [`waɪnərɪ]	釀酒廠
culture [`kʌltʃə]	文化
agency [`edʒənsɪ]	代辦處，經銷處
heritage [`hɛrətɪdʒ]	遺產，世襲財產
museum [mju`zɪəm]	博物館
tourist [`tʊrɪst]	旅遊者，觀光者
theater [`θɪətə]	劇場；電影院
guide [gaɪd]	嚮導，導遊；指南
place [ples]	地方，地點
authentic [ɔ`θɛntɪk]	可信的，真實的；真正的
cuisine [kwɪ`zin]	烹飪；烹調法；菜餚

❼
觀光篇

track 68

7.3 問路

會話實例

A Excuse me. Could you tell me how to get to the fish market?

不好意思，可以麻煩你跟我說要怎麼去魚市場嗎？

B You can take a bus or go by walking.

你可以搭巴士或走路去。

A How long is the walk?

走路要多久？

B Well...about 15 minutes.

嗯...大概十五分鐘。

A Can you show me the direction?

你可以跟我講怎麼去嗎？

B Go down this street, when you reach the post office, turn right. Keep walking for about 5 minutes, it will be on your left.

沿著這條街直走，到達郵局後右轉。繼續走大概五分鐘，魚市場就在你的左手邊。

A Thank you very much!

謝謝你！

B My pleasure.
　不客氣。

延伸例句

▶ How can I get to the botanic garden?
　請問植物園要怎麼走？

▶ Would you mind telling me how I can get to
　the city library?
　可以麻煩你跟我說要如何去市立圖書館嗎？

▶ How can I get to the train station?
　火車站要怎麼走？

▶ Which bus should I take?
　我要搭幾號公車？

▶ How long is it going to take to get there?
　要花多久時間？

▶ Go up this street.
　沿著這條路走。

▶ Go along this street.
　沿著這條路走。

▶ Turn left at the next intersection.
　下個十字路口左轉。

▶ When you reach the convenience store, turn left.
　你到達便利商店後，左轉。

▶ It is around the corner.
轉個彎就到了。

相關單字、片語

market [ˋmɑrkɪt]	市場
show [ʃo]	告知；指出
post office	郵局
post [post]	郵政（制度）；郵寄
office [ˋɔfɪs]	辦公室
botanic [boˋtænɪk]	植物的；植物學的
garden [ˋgɑrdn]	花園；菜園
along [əˋlɔŋ]	沿著；順著
intersection [ˏɪntəˋsɛkʃən]	十字路口
around [əˋraʊnd]	圍繞，環繞；在……四處

track 69

7.4 名勝古蹟景點

會話實例

Ⓐ Excuse me, what's that building?
不好意思，那是什麼建築？

Ⓑ It's the city library.
市立圖書館。

A Isn't it beautiful?

好漂亮啊！

B Yea, it's one of the iconic buildings in the city.

對呀，這是城市裡最具代表性的建築之一。

A When was it built?

他是什麼時候蓋的？

B It was built in 19 century.

十九世紀。

A Can I visit if I'm not a member?

如果沒有會員可以參觀嗎？

B Yes, you just have to sign in at the reception.

可以，你只需要在接待台簽到。

延伸例句

▶ I'd like to visit some historical sites.
我想要參觀歷史遺跡。

▶ What are the cultural heritage sites here?
這裡有哪些人文歷史遺跡？

▶ We went to visit the Carthage ruins.
我們去參觀卡太基遺址。

▶ It's one of the largest mosques in the world.
這是全世界最大的清真寺。

▶ This is the iconic building of the architect.
這是這位建築師的代表性作品。

▶ This beautiful cathedral is Moscow's most visited tourist attraction.
這座美麗的大教堂是莫斯科最多遊客觀光的景點。

▶ The cathedral was built between 1555 and 1561.
這座大教堂是在1555年到1561年間建設的。

▶ The temple was destroyed twice and rebuilt each time.
這座神殿曾經被摧毀兩次，並在每次被摧毀後歷經重建。

▶ The Roman Colosseum is the largest building remaining from Roman times.
羅馬競技場是從羅馬時期遺留到現在的最大建築。

相關單字、片語

iconic [aɪ`kɑnɪk]	代表性的
build [bɪld]	建築；造
century [`sɛntʃʊrɪ]	世紀；一百年
reception [rɪ`sɛpʃən]	接待處
historical [hɪs`tɔrɪk!]	歷史的，史學的
site [saɪt]	舊址，遺跡
cultural [`kʌltʃərəl]	文化的；人文的
ruin [`rʊɪn]	廢墟；遺跡

mosque [mɑsk]	清真寺，回教寺院
architect [ˋɑrkəˌtɛkt]	建築師；設計師
cathedral [kəˋθidrəl]	大教堂
attraction [əˋtrækʃən]	吸引物；喜聞樂見的事物
temple [ˋtɛmp!]	神殿，聖堂；（佛教的）寺院，寺廟
Colosseum [ˌkɑləˋsiəm]	古羅馬圓形大競技場
remain [rɪˋmen]	剩下，餘留；繼續存在

8

休閒娛樂篇

看電影

會話實例

A What are you up to tonight?
你今晚要做什麼？

B Not much.
沒有要幹嘛。

A Do you want to go see a movie with me?
你要不要跟我去看電影？

B Yea, what's on now?
好呀，現在有什麼電影上映？

A Let me see…what about this one? It's a comedy.
讓我看看...這個如何？是一部喜劇。

B Can you show me the trailer?.
我可以看預告片嗎？

A Yea, here you go.
好啊，給你。

B It's funny! Let's go for this one!
看起來好好笑！我們去看這部吧！

延伸例句

▷ What type of movies do you like?
你喜歡什麼類型的電影？

▷ My favorite type of movie is animation.
我最喜歡的電影類型是動畫片。

▷ I like action films.
我喜歡動作片。

▷ I like drama and horror movies.
我喜歡劇情片跟恐怖片。

▷ I don't like musical movies.
我不喜歡歌舞片。

▷ What's your favorite movie?
你最喜歡哪部電影？

▷ Who's the director of this movie?
這部電影的導演是誰？

▷ The producer of this movie is very famous.
這部電影的製作人非常著名。

▷ I really love this actor.
我真的很喜歡這個演員。

▷ I like the soundtrack.
我很喜歡電影原聲帶。

相關單字、片語

comedy [ˈkɑmədɪ]	喜劇
trailer [ˈtrelɚ]	電影預告片;預告節目
funny [ˈfʌnɪ]	有趣的;滑稽可笑的
animation [͵ænəˈmeʃən]	卡通片,動畫片
action [ˈækʃən]	行動;行為;活動
film [fɪlm]	電影
drama [ˈdrɑmə]	戲,戲劇;戲劇性事件;戲劇性
horror [ˈhɔrɚ]	恐怖,震驚
musical [ˈmjuzɪk!]	音樂的
favorite [ˈfevərɪt]	特別喜愛的人（或物）
producer [prəˈdjusɚ]	生產者,製造者
famous [ˈfeməs]	著名的,出名的
actor [ˈæktɚ]	男演員;演員
soundtrack [ˈsaʊnd͵træk]	聲帶;電影配音

track 71

8.2

聽音樂

會話實例

A What are you listening to?

你在聽什麼音樂？

8 休閒娛樂篇

2
7
1

B It's R&B. The artist is called Aimee.
這是節奏藍調，歌手叫做艾米。

A I like the melody of this song.
我喜歡這首歌的旋律。

B She's my favorite singer.
這是我最喜歡的歌手。

A Did you buy her album?
你有買她的專輯嗎？

B Yes, I have 4 of her albums.
有呀，我有四張她的專輯。

A Can I borrow some?
我可以借一些嗎？

B Yes, of course.
當然可以。

延伸例句

▶ I'm going to a music festival.
我要去參加音樂節。

▶ I bought the ticket for this concert.
我買了這場音樂會的票。

▶ They have a gig at the bar.
他們在酒吧舉行一場演出。

▶ Do you play any instruments?
你會任何樂器嗎？

▶ What instrument do you play?
你會什麼樂器？

▶ I like to play guitar.
我喜歡彈吉他。

▶ I'm the vocalist in the band.
我是樂團裡的主唱。

▶ I play drums.
我打鼓。

▶ What kind of music do you like to listen to?
你喜歡聽什麼樣的音樂？

▶ I like jazz and hip hop.
我喜歡爵士跟嘻哈音樂。

▶ I listen to all different types of music.
我喜歡聽各種不同類型的音樂。

▶ Today, many people stream their favorite music from online services.
現今有許多人們從線上音樂串流服務下載他們最喜歡的音樂。

▶ Streaming is the most common way to listen to music.
串流音樂是聽音樂最常見的方式。

相關單字、片語

listen [`lɪsn]	聽，留神聽
artist [`artɪst]	藝人
melody [`mɛlədɪ]	旋律；主調
song [sɔŋ]	歌，歌曲
singer [`sɪŋɚ]	歌唱家，歌手
album [`ælbəm]	一套唱片；一套錄音帶
festival [`fɛstəv!]	節日，喜慶日
concert [`kansɚt]	音樂會，演奏會
gig [gɪg]	（爵士樂、搖滾樂等）演奏，公演
instrument [`ɪnstrəmənt]	器械；樂器
guitar [gɪ`tar]	吉他
dead [lid]	最重要的；領先的
vocalist [`vokəlɪst]	歌手；歌唱家；聲樂家
band [bænd]	樂隊
drum [drʌm]	鼓
jazz [dʒæz]	爵士樂（舞）
hip hop	嘻哈音樂
stream [strim]	流出；湧出；使飄動

看球賽

會話實例

Ⓐ Do you like basketball?
你喜歡籃球嗎？

Ⓑ Yes.
喜歡。

Ⓐ Do you wanna go see a match with me tomorrow?
你明天要不要跟我去看比賽？

Ⓑ I'd love to. What time?
好呀，什麼時候？

Ⓐ Tomorrow evening at 7pm.
明天晚上七點。

Ⓑ Yea, sure.
好。

Ⓐ Great, I'll see you at the stadium.
太好了，那明天體育館見。

Ⓑ See you tomorrow!
明天見！

延伸例句

▶ Did you watch the U.S. Open Tennis Championships?
你有看美網公開賽嗎？

▶ Did you watch the badminton tournament yesterday?
你昨天有看羽毛球錦標賽嗎？

▶ I like to watch table tennis matches on TV.
我喜歡在電視上看桌球比賽。

▶ I enjoy watching football matches with friends in the bars.
我喜歡和朋友在酒吧看足球比賽。

▶ How much does it cost to go to a baseball game?
去看棒球比賽要多少錢？

▶ What are the upcoming cricket matches?
接下來有什麼板球比賽？

▶ What time does the Golf Tournament of Championships start?
高爾夫球冠軍賽幾點開始？

▶ Rugby is a popular sport in South Africa.
英式橄欖球在南非是很受歡迎的運動。

▶ Do you want to join the volleyball team?
　你要不要加入排球隊？

相關單字、片語

stadium [ˋstedɪəm]	體育場，運動場
watch [wɑtʃ]	觀看；注視
open [ˋopən]	公開賽
tennis [ˋtɛnɪs]	網球（運動）
championship [ˋtʃæmpɪənˏʃɪp]	冠軍的地位，冠軍稱號；錦標賽
tournament [ˋtɝnəmənt]	比賽；錦標賽；聯賽
football [ˋfʊtˏbɔl]	橄欖球；足球
baseball [ˋbesˏbɔl]	棒球運動
upcoming [ˋʌpˏkʌmɪŋ]	即將來臨的
cricket [ˋkrɪkɪt]	板球
golf [gɑlf]	高爾夫球運動
rugby [ˋrʌgbɪ]	英式橄欖球
sport [sport]	運動，體育競技活動
talented [ˋtæləntɪd]	有天才的，有才幹的
volleyball [ˋvɑlɪˏbɔl]	排球
team [tim]	隊；組；班

🎧 track 73

8.4

去游泳

會話實例

A What plans do you have for summer vacation?

你暑假有什麼計畫？

B I want to learn how to swim.

我想要學會游泳。

A Maybe my brother can teach you.

或許我哥可以教你。

B Really? That'd be great.

真的嗎？太好了。

A He's very good at teaching, plus, he is a qualified lifeguard.

他很會教人，加上他是合格救生員。

B Awesome!

太棒了！

A Do you want to come swim with us tomorrow?

你明天要不要來跟我們游泳？

B Ok! I have to find out where my goggles are.

好！我得要把我的蛙鏡找出來。

延伸例句

▶ Let's warm up before jumping into the pool!

下水前，我們先來暖身！

▶ My mom can only do breaststroke.

我媽媽只會游蛙式。

▶ Is butterfly faster than freestyle?

游蝶式比自由式快嗎？

▶ Can you teach me how to do backstroke?

你可以教我游仰式嗎？

▶ I can do front crawl.

我會捷泳。

▶ That was very brave of you to swim across the lake.

你能泳渡這座湖真是勇敢。

▶ I don't like to swim in open water.

我不喜歡在開放水域游泳。

▶ What to do if I get cramps while swimming?

如果我在游泳時抽筋要怎麼辦？

▶ Can you throw the kickboard to me?
　你可以把浮板丟給我嗎？

相關單字、片語

learn [lɝn]	學習；學會
swim [swɪm]	游，游泳
teach [titʃ]	教，講授
qualified [`kwɑləˌfaɪd]	具備必要條件的；合格的；勝任的
plus [plʌs]	加，加上；外加
lifeguard [`laɪfˌgɑrd]	救生員
awesome [`ɔsəm]	令人驚嘆的；使人驚懼的
goggles [`gɑglz]	護目鏡；蛙鏡
warm up	加熱，變暖；做準備；(使)更活躍
jump [dʒʌmp]	跳；跳躍
pool [pul]	水塘，水池
breaststroke [`brɛstˌstrok]	(游泳) 俯泳，蛙式泳
butterfly [`bʌtɚˌflaɪ]	蝶泳
freestyle [`friˌstaɪl]	(游泳等) 自由式的
backstroke [`bækˌstrok]	反擊；仰泳
front [frʌnt]	前面的；正面
crawl [krɔl]	爬泳，自由式游泳
brave [brev]	勇敢的，英勇的
across [ə`krɔs]	橫越，穿過

lake [lek]	湖
cramp [kræmp]	抽筋
throw [θro]	投，擲，拋，扔

  track 74

8.5 滑雪溜冰

會話實例

Ⓐ My family and I are going to a ski resort in France for Christmas.
我家人和我要去法國的滑雪勝地過聖誕節。

Ⓑ That's awesome!
好棒！

Ⓐ Yea, we're so excited.
對呀，我們很興奮。

Ⓑ How long are you gonna stay?
你們要去幾天？

Ⓐ 7 days.
七天。

Ⓑ Do you snowboard or ski?
你滑單板還是雙板？

Ⓐ I can only ski, but I want to learn snowboarding.

我只會滑雙板，但是我想要學單板滑雪。

Ⓑ I'm sure that you can do it!

我相信你能辦到的！

延伸例句

▶ I love winter activities such as ice skating and skiing.

我很愛冬季運動，像是溜冰跟滑雪。

▶ She got a new pair of skates.

她得到一雙新的溜冰鞋。

▶ We're going skiing during winter vacation.

我們寒假要去滑雪。

▶ Do I have to own my equipment?

我需要有自己的裝備嗎？

▶ I'd like to take ski lessons.

我想要上滑雪課。

▶ I'd like to buy salopettes for skiing.

我要買滑雪用的背帶褲。

▶ I want to buy new goggles and gloves for skiing.

我想要買新的滑雪護目鏡跟手套。

► Skiing off-piste can be dangerous.
在滑雪道外滑雪很危險。

► Is snowboarding or skiing easier for beginners?
對初學者來說,雙板滑雪還是單板滑雪比較簡單?

相關單字、片語

ski [ski]	滑雪;滑雪屐
resort [rɪˋzɔrt]	常去的休閒度假之處;名勝
stay [ste]	停留;留下;暫住
snowboard [ˋsno͵bord]	用滑雪板滑雪;單板滑雪
activity [ækˋtɪvətɪ]	活動;活動力
skate [sket]	滑冰,溜冰;冰鞋;
	四輪溜冰鞋
pair [pɛr]	一對,一雙
during [ˋdjʊrɪŋ]	在……的整個期間
own [on]	有,擁有
equipment [ɪˋkwɪpmənt]	配備,裝備
lesson [ˋlɛsn]	功課;課業;課程
glove [glʌv]	手套
off-piste [ˋɔf͵pist]	在滑雪道外的
dangerous [ˋdendʒərəs]	危險的;不安全的
easy [ˋizɪ]	容易的;不費力的
beginner [bɪˋgɪnɚ]	初學者,新手

🎧 track 75

8.6 野餐露營

會話實例

Ⓐ We're planning for a camping trip in April.

我們在計劃四月去露營旅行。

Ⓑ Where are you camping?

你們要去哪裡露營?

Ⓐ We want to camp in Arches National Park in Utah.

我們想去猶他州的拱門國家公園露營。

Ⓑ Wow! That must be fun!

哇!一定會很好玩!

Ⓐ Do you want to join us?

你要加入我們嗎?

Ⓑ Sure! It's just that I don't have any camping gear.

好呀!但是我沒有任何露營裝備。

Ⓐ Don't worry, we have most of them. You just need to bring a sleeping bag.

別擔心,我們有大部分的裝備,你只需要帶你的睡袋。

B Great! I'll go buy one.
太好了！我會去買。

延伸例句

▶ Camping became very popular these years.
露營近年來變得非常熱門。

▶ We rented a camper van for our road trip.
我們租了一台露營車去公路旅行。

▶ What equipment comes with the camper van?
露營車上有什麼設備？

▶ How much does it cost to rent a camper van?
租一台露營車要多少錢？

▶ We camped in the mountains.
我們在山上露營。

▶ We set up our camp at the beach.
我們在海灘紮營。

▶ We pitched our tent by the river.
我們在河邊搭帳篷。

▶ It's getting cold. Let's build a campfire.
變冷了，我們來搭營火吧。

▶ I borrowed these camp chairs from my friend.
我跟朋友借了這些露營用的椅子。

相關單字、片語

camp [kæmp]	紮營；宿營；露營
gear [gɪr]	工具；設備，裝置
sleeping bag	睡袋
van [væn]	有蓋小貨車；箱形客貨兩用車
mountain [ˈmaʊntn]	山；山脈
beach [bitʃ]	海灘
pitch [pɪtʃ]	搭（帳篷）；紮（營）
river [ˈrɪvɚ]	江，河
campfire [ˈkæmpˌfaɪr]	營火，篝火；營火會

🎧 track 76

8.7 動物園

會話實例

A My son's birthday is coming up.

我兒子生日快到了。

B How are you going to celebrate?

你們要怎麼慶祝？

A I don't know yet, I bought him a present. But I want to do something with him.

我還不知道耶，我買了個禮物要給他，但我想跟他一起做點什麼。

B Why don't you take him to the zoo?
你何不帶他去動物園？

A Thanks! That's a great idea!
謝拉！真是個好主意！

B Right? Children love zoos.
對吧？孩子都愛動物園。

A I'll take him to the zoo. He loves animals.
我會帶他去動物園，他超愛動物。

延伸例句

▶ What are the opening hours of Taipei Zoo?
我想知道台北動物園的開門時間？

▶ I'd like to book a zoo guided tour for 10 people.
我想要預訂動物園導覽團，我們有十個人。

▶ Let's go see the Amphibian and Reptile House!
我們去看兩棲爬蟲動物館！

▶ Penguin house is the most popular section in the zoo.
企鵝館是動物園裡最受歡迎的區。

▶ We went to visit the wildlife sanctuary in Queensland, They take care of injured or orphaned animals.
我們去參觀昆士蘭的野生動物庇護所，他們照顧受傷或失去母獸的動物。

▶ Zookeepers are responsible for feeding animals and cleaning their enclosure.
動物管理員要負責餵食動物並且清理牠們的圍欄。

▶ We brought our kids to an animal art workshop in the zoo.
我們帶孩子去動物園裡的動物藝術創作坊。

▶ Please do not feed the animals.
請勿餵食動物。

▶ Do not sit, climb or lean on fences.
請勿坐、爬或靠在圍籬上。

▶ They have free wheelchair and stroller services in the zoo.
動物園提供輪椅及娃娃車的免費租借服務。

▶ What itinerary do you recommend?
你有建議的遊覽路線嗎？

▶ Can I re-enter the park after exiting?
我可以在離開後又重新進入園區嗎？

▶ Are lockers available at the Visitor Center?
旅客中心有提供置物櫃服務嗎？

▶ Is smoking prohibited at the zoo?
動物園裡禁止吸菸嗎？

▶ Can I use flash when shooting animals?
拍動物的時候可以用閃光燈嗎？

相關單字、片語

zoo [zu]	動物園
animal [ˋænəm!]	動物；獸
amphibian [æmˋfɪbɪən]	兩棲（類）的；水陸兩用的
penguin [ˋpɛngwɪn]	企鵝
reptile [ˋrɛpt!]	爬行動物；爬蟲類
wildlife [ˋwaɪld͵laɪf]	野生生物的
sanctuary [ˋsæŋktʃʊɛrɪ]	庇護所，避難所
injure [ˋɪndʒɚ]	傷害；損害；毀壞
orphan [ˋɔrfən]	無雙親的，無父(或母)的，孤兒的；(幼小動物) 失去母獸的
zookeeper [ˋzu͵kipɚ]	動物園管理員
responsible [rɪˋspɑnsəb!]	需負責任的，承擔責任的
enclosure [ɪnˋkloʒɚ]	圍欄，圍牆
workshop [ˋwɝ͵kʃɑp]	工場；作坊
climb [klaɪm]	爬，攀登
lean [lin]	傾斜；傾身
fence [fɛns]	柵欄；籬笆
itinerary [aɪˋtɪnə͵rɛrɪ]	旅程；路線；旅行計畫
locker [ˋlɑkɚ]	衣物櫃
visitor [ˋvɪzɪtɚ]	觀光者；參觀者
prohibit [prəˋhɪbɪt]	禁止
flash [flæʃ]	閃光攝影術；閃光燈
shoot [ʃut]	拍攝

旅遊英文 一點通

8.8 去遊樂園

會話實例

A What's your favorite facility so far?
你目前最喜歡哪個設施？

B That will definitely be the pirate ship!
絕對是海盜船。

A It was really exciting, but I got so dizzy after taking it.
真的很刺激，但我玩完之後頭很暈。

B Are you ok? Do you need some more water?
你還好嗎？你還需要水嗎？

A I'm alright after sitting down at the rest area.
我在休息區坐一下後好多了。

B What about you? What's your favorite?
你呢？你最喜歡哪個？

A I love the bumper car! Do you want to ride again?
我超愛碰碰車！你想再玩一次嗎？

B Yea!
好呀！

延伸例句

▶ The amusement park is open year-round.
遊樂園整年都有開。

▶ This amusement park has the best roller coaster.
這家遊樂園有最棒的雲霄飛車。

▶ What country has the fastest roller coaster?
哪個國家的雲霄飛車最快？

▶ There are many theme parks in Orlando.
奧蘭多有很多的主題遊樂公園。

▶ What time is the parade?
遊行什麼時候開始？

▶ John proposed to his girlfriend while riding on the Ferris wheel.
約翰在摩天輪上和女友求婚。

▶ Do you want to go ride the merry-go-round?
你要不要去玩旋轉木馬？

▶ Let's go to the souvenir shop!
我們去逛紀念品店！

▶ We had queued for two hours.
我們排隊排了兩個小時了。

8 休閒娛樂篇

▶ We had a good time at Disney theme park even though it was raining.

即使下雨，我們還是在迪士尼樂園玩得很愉快。

▶ We both feel emotional after watching the classic cartoon in the children's theater.

我們在兒童劇院看完經典卡通後都感到感動。

▶ There are lockers in the park for visitors to deposit their personal belongings.

園區內有置物櫃讓遊客可以寄放個人物品。

▶ There are charging sockets at the Visitor Center.

訪客中心有充電插座。

▶ Drinking fountains with chilled and warm water are available in the park.

園區有提供冷、溫水飲用水噴泉。

▶ There are four nursing rooms by the Visitor Center.

遊客中心旁邊有四個哺乳室。

相關單字、片語

definitely [ˋdɛfənɪtlɪ]	明確地；明顯地，清楚地；肯定地；當然
pirate [ˋpaɪrət]	海盜；劫掠者；海盜船
exciting [ɪkˋsaɪtɪŋ]	令人興奮的；令人激動的

bumper [`bʌmpə-]	緩衝器；減震物；（汽車前後的）保險槓
amusement [ə`mjuzmənt]	娛樂，消遣；娛樂活動
year-round [`jɪr,raʊnd]	整年的
roller [`rolə-]	滾動物；滾柱；滾筒
coaster [`kostə-]	沿岸貿易船；（滑坡用的）橇，雪橇
roller coaster	雲霄飛車
parade [pə`red]	行進，行列，遊行
propose [prə`poz]	求婚
girlfriend [`gɜ-l,frɛnd]	女朋友
Ferris	
費理斯（十九世紀美國工程師，發明一種轉輪）	
merry-go-round [`mɛrɪgo,raʊnd]	
	旋轉木馬
theme [θim]	主題
even [`ivən]	甚至；連
even if	即使
classic [`klæsɪk]	經典的
cartoon [kɑr`tun]	卡通電影，卡通
emotional [ɪ`moʃən!]	易動情的；感情脆弱的
socket [`sɑkɪt]	插座；插口
chilled [tʃɪld]	冷的，涼颼颼的
nurse [nɜ-s]	當……的褓姆；給……餵奶

track 78

8.9 逛美術館、博物館

會話實例

A The Louvre museum is huge!

羅浮宮好大！

B Yea, it's difficult to find everything.

對呀，要找到所有的束西有點困難。

A Let's check the floor plan.

我們來看看樓層圖。

B Didn't you take a museum brochure?

你沒有拿導覽手冊嗎？

A No, sorry, I forgot.

沒，抱歉，我忘記了。

B Would you like to start with Sully Wing? There are many ancient Egyptian artifacts.

你想從敘利館開始參觀嗎？這裡有很多埃及古文物。

A Sounds good.

聽起來不錯。

B Let's go!

走吧！

延伸例句

▶ We went to more than 5 museums during our stay in Paris.
在巴黎旅行的時候，我們去了超過五個博物館。

▶ May I know which way is to the art gallery?
請問美術館要怎麼走？

▶ How did you like the museum visit?
你喜歡這次的博物館之旅嗎？

▶ What exhibitions are on in London?
倫敦現在有什麼展覽？

▶ We plan to visit the contemporary art museum.
我們計畫要去當代藝術美術館。

▶ These sculptures are so delicate.
這些雕刻品非常精美。

▶ How much is the admission fee for the modern art museum?
現代藝術美術館的門票要多少？

▶ This is my favorite oil painting.
這是我最喜歡的一幅油畫。

▶ We provide exhibition tour services, you just have to download this app.
我們有提供展覽導覽服務，您只需下載此應用程式。

旅遊英文一點通

- ▶ We also have guided tours for groups.
  我們也有提供團體導覽服務。

- ▶ We open from 10am to 5pm.
  我們從早上十點開到下午五點。

- ▶ Please do not use flash-light.
  請勿使用閃光燈。

- ▶ Please help keep our facilities clean.
  請協助保持設施清潔。

- ▶ Do not eat / drink beyond the designated areas of the museum.
  請勿在博物館的指定區域之外飲食。

- ▶ Please help maintain a quiet and pleasant environment.
  請協助保持安靜且怡人的環境。

相關單字、片語

huge [hjudʒ]	龐大的；巨大的
booklet [`buklɪt]	小冊子
ancient [`enʃənt]	古代的；古老的
Egyptian [ɪ`dʒɪpʃən]	埃及的
artifact [`ɑrtɪˌfækt]	工藝品；手工藝品
gallery [`gælərɪ]	畫廊，美術館
exhibition [ˌɛksə`bɪʃən]	展覽；展覽會
contemporary [kən`tɛmpəˌrɛrɪ]	當代的

sculpture [ˋskʌlptʃə]	雕刻品，雕塑品；雕像
delicate [ˋdɛləkət]	精美的，雅緻的
admission [ədˋmɪʃən]	入場費；入場券，門票
modern [ˋmadən]	現代的；近代的
modern art	現代藝術
oil painting	油畫；油畫藝術
painting [ˋpentɪŋ]	繪畫；繪畫藝術
group [grup]	集體；團體
clean [klin]	清潔的；未汙染的
beyond [bɪˋjɑnd]	（指範圍）越出
quiet [ˋkwaɪət]	安靜的；輕聲的
pleasant [ˋplɛzənt]	令人愉快的；舒適的
environment [ɪnˋvaɪrənmənt]	環境；四周狀況

track 79

8.10
養寵物

會話實例

A We decided to bring two stray puppies home.

我們決定要帶兩隻流浪幼犬回家。

B Really? Where did you find them?

真的嗎？你們在哪裡找到牠們的？

Ⓐ We found them while they were trying to cross the street during rush hour.

我們找到牠們的時候，牠們嘗試在尖峰時刻過馬路。

Ⓑ Oh, that's dangerous for them!

噢，真危險！

Ⓐ They must be scared.

牠們一定很害怕。

Ⓑ Are you going to bring them to the vet?

你要帶牠們去看獸醫嗎？

Ⓐ Yes, we'll go after Howard finishes his work.

會，等霍爾下班後，我們會去。

Ⓑ Yea, it's better to do a checkup.

嗯，最好做個檢查。

延伸例句

▶ I'm taking my dog for a walk.

我在遛狗。

▶ I take my cat to the groomer once a month.

我每個月會帶我的貓去寵物美容。

▶ This is my dog, Nico, she's one year old and very energetic.

這是我的狗，尼可，她現在一歲，非常有活力。

▶ I have to take my dogs to the vet for vaccinations.
  我要帶我的狗狗們去獸醫打疫苗。

▶ I want to buy a new leash for my dog.
  我想要幫我的狗買新的鏈條。

▶ My dog opened the drawer by itself and ate all the treats.
  我的狗自己打開抽屜然後把所有的零食都吃掉了。

▶ My neighbor has a parrot as a pet.
  我的鄰居養鸚鵡當寵物。

▶ How often do I need to clear the cat litter tray?
  我多久該清一次貓砂盆？

▶ We can go to a pet friendly restaurant.
  我們可以去寵物友善餐廳。

相關單字、片語

stray [stre]	迷路的，走失的；流浪的
puppy [ˋpʌpɪ]	小狗，幼犬
cross [krɔs]	越過，渡過
rush hour [skerd]	（上下班時）交通擁擠時間；尖峰時間
scared	吃驚的，嚇壞的；恐懼的
vet [vɛt]	獸醫
finish [ˋfɪnɪʃ]	結束；完成

checkup [ˋtʃɛkˌʌp]	檢查;核對;體格檢查
groom [grum]	使整潔;打扮
energetic [ˌɛnɚˋdʒɛtɪk]	精力旺盛的;精神飽滿的
vaccination [ˌvæksnˋeʃən]	疫苗接種
leash [liʃ]	皮帶,鏈條
drawer [ˋdrɔɚ]	抽屜
treat [trit]	請客,款待;美食
parrot [ˋpærət]	鸚鵡
clear [klɪr]	變乾淨;變清澈
litter [ˋlɪtɚ]	廢棄物,零亂之物
tray [tre]	盤子,托盤
friendly [ˋfrɛndlɪ]	友好的,親切的

🎧 track 80

8.11 烹飪

會話實例

A How may I help you today?
你需要幫忙嗎?

B I'm looking for ingredients for a dinner party.
我在找晚餐派對的食材。

Ⓐ What is on your menu?
你要做什麼菜？

Ⓑ I will make a meat and cheese platter, salad, potato gratin, lamb chops and tiramisu for dessert.
我會準備冷肉及起司盤、沙拉、烤奶油馬鈴薯、羊排、提拉米蘇作為甜點。

Ⓐ That sounds yummy! Let me show you some cheese and salami.
聽起來很美味！我來幫你介紹起司跟薩拉米香腸。

Ⓑ Great! I'll also need some nuts.
太好了！我還需要一些堅果。

Ⓐ No problem!
沒問題！

延伸例句

▶ I like baking.
我喜歡烘培。

▶ I like cooking.
我喜歡烹飪。

▶ I'm applying for culinary schools.
我在申請廚藝學校。

▶ I enjoy watching cooking programs.
我喜歡看烹飪節目。

▶ Katsu Curry is my favorite dish.
炸雞排咖哩是我最愛吃的菜。

▶ This homemade garlic bread is so delicious.
這個自製大蒜麵包非常美味。

▶ I made breakfast for us.
我幫我們做了早餐。

▶ Sammy went to a cooking class to learn Thai cuisine.
珊米去烹飪課學做泰式料理。

▶ We went to a sushi making class in Tokyo.
我們在東京的時候去上了學做壽司的課。

▶ Do you know a good recipe for quiche?
你知道好吃的法式鹹派的食譜？

▶ Do you know how to make Caesar dressing from scratch?
你知道要如何自己做凱薩沙拉醬嗎？

▶ Lisa held a cooking party last weekend.
麗莎上週末辦了煮飯派對。

▶ Grilling is the technique of cooking foods over direct heat.
燒烤是一種將食物放在直接熱源上烹煮的方式。

相關單字、片語

ingredient [ɪnˋgrɪdɪənt]	（烹調的）原料
dinner [ˋdɪnə]	晚餐；正餐
meat [mit]	（食用的）肉
platter [ˋplætə]	大淺盤（通常為橢圓形）
gratin [ˋgrætæn]	【法】奶油烤菜
lamb [læm]	小羊；羔羊肉
chop [tʃɑp]	肋骨肉，排骨；砍，劈，剁
tiramisu [ˌtɪrəmiˋsu]	提拉米蘇
dessert [dɪˋzɝt]	甜點心；餐後甜點
yummy [ˋjʌmɪ]	好吃的；美味的
salami [səˋlɑmɪ]	薩拉米香腸（義大利蒜味香腸）
nut [nʌt]	堅果；核果
baking [ˋbekɪŋ]	烘焙，烘烤
cooking [ˋkʊkɪŋ]	烹調；烹調術；飯菜
culinary [ˋkjulɪˌnɛrɪ]	烹飪的
program [ˋprogræm]	節目，表演
dish [dɪʃ]	一盤菜；菜餚
homemade [ˋhomˋmed]	自製的；家裡做的
garlic [ˋgɑrlɪk]	大蒜；蒜頭
breakfast [ˋbrɛkfəst]	早餐，早飯
class [klæs]	課；上課
sushi [ˋsuʃɪ]	壽司
making [ˋmekɪŋ]	製造；組合；形成；一次的製造量

recipe [ˋrɛsəpɪ]	烹飪法;食譜
quiche [kiʃ]	（加有切碎之火腿、海鮮或蔬菜等的）乳蛋餅
from scratch	從零開始;從頭做起
scratch [skrætʃ]	起跑線;刮痕;抓痕;擦傷
grill [grɪl]	烤架;燒烤的肉類食物
technique [tɛkˋnik]	技巧;技術;技法【口】手段,方法
direct [dəˋrɛkt]	直接的

9

辦公室篇

請假

會話實例

A How are you, Jimmy?

你好嗎，吉米？

B Hello, Daniel. I'm calling to inform you that I can't make it to work today, as I've come down with a fever.

哈囉，丹尼爾，我打來通知你我發燒了，今天無法上班。

A Oh, Are you alright?

喔，你還好嗎？

B I feel pretty bad. I think it's best for me to take the day off and rest so I can come back tomorrow.

我感到糟透了，我想我最好請一天假在家充分休息，明天才能回去上班。

A I see, I'll ask Amy to handle your workload.

我瞭解了，我會請艾咪協助處理你的工作。

B Thanks. I'll try to be on email as much as I can.

謝啦，我會盡量回覆電子郵件。

9 辦公室篇

A Don't worry, buddy. Just take good care of yourself and rest.

別擔心，老兄，好好照顧自己、好好休息。

B Thanks for your understanding.

多謝你的理解。

延伸例句

▶ I'd like to take personal leave tomorrow.

我明天想請事假。

▶ I wonder if I could have a day off tomorrow.

我能否明天請一天假？

▶ Could I have three days off next week?

我下週能請三天假嗎？

▶ Lauren will be away on maternity leave for 3 months.

羅蘭將休三個月產假。

▶ David is going to take two weeks paternity leave.

大衛要請兩禮拜的陪產假。

▶ Annie called in sick this morning.

安妮今天早上請病假。

▶ He is off today.

他今天請假。

▶ Helen had three personal days off last week.
海倫上禮拜請了三天事假。

▶ I'd like to take annual leave for a vacation in Europe.
我想要請年假去歐洲度假。

▶ I have a doctor's appointment on the schedule for Thursday, so I'll be out of the office then.
我禮拜四有預約看診日程，所以我到時不會在辦公室。

▶ I'm not feeling well and I need to use a sick day. I'll be back tomorrow.
我感覺不太舒服，我需要請病假，我明天再進辦公室。

▶ My son fell ill this morning and I need to take him to the doctor. I'll have to use a sick day and come back tomorrow.
我兒子早上不舒服，我必須帶他去看醫生，我今天請病假，明天再進辦公室。

▶ I will be back in the office as early as I can.
我會儘早回到辦公室。

▶ I apologize for any inconvenience.
造成任何困擾，我感到很抱歉。

▶ I appreciate your understanding.
感謝你的理解。

▶ I got unpaid leave for 2 months.
我有兩個月無薪假。

▶ Employees are entitled to an annual paid leave of thirty days.
職員一年可享受三十天帶薪的假期。

相關單字、片語

pretty [`prɪtɪ]	相當，頗，很，非常
rest up	得到充分休息；養足精神
handle [`hænd!]	操作；操縱；指揮；管理
workload [`wɝk,lod]	工作量
understanding [,ʌndə`stændɪŋ]	了解；理解
leave [liv]	休假；休假期
maternity [mə`tɝnɪtɪ]	適用於孕婦的；產婦的
paternity leave	得新生兒後的）父親假
paternity [pə`tɝnɪtɪ]	父權；父子關係；父親的義務
doctor [`dɑktə]	醫生，醫師
annual [`ænjʊəl]	一年的；一年一次的；每年的；全年的
appointment [ə`pɔɪntmənt]	約定
ill [ɪl]	生病的，不健康的
unpaid [ʌn`ped]	無報酬的
employee [ɛmplɔɪ`i]	受僱者，僱工，僱員，從業員工
entitle [ɪn`taɪt!]	給……權力（或資格）
paid [ped]	有薪金的

交換名片

會話實例

A Mr. Lin. It was nice talking to you today.
林先生,今天很開心可以跟您談話。

B Same here, Mr. Wang. Nice to meet you.
我也是,王先生,非常開心能認識您。

A I look forward to visiting your company and talking more about the project.
我很期待去您的公司拜訪,並且討論更多計畫的細節。

B Me, too. Could I have your contact number?
我也是,我可以跟您要聯絡電話嗎?

A Yea, sure, here's my business card.
當然,這是我的名片。

B Here you go, here's mine. Let's stay in touch.
給您,這是我的,我們保持聯絡。

A I'll send you more information.
我會寄更多資訊給您。

9 辦公室篇

B Thank you.
謝謝。

延伸例句

▶ Could you please give me the details?
你可以給我細節嗎？

▶ Would it be possible for me to get more details?
可以請你可以給我更多細節嗎？

▶ I'd love to talk to you personally. Would you send me your phone number, please?
我想親自與你談話，你可以告訴我的電話號碼嗎？

▶ I would like to request you to kindly provide our organisation with the contact details of your client Dr Alex Jenkins.
懇請您提供您的客戶阿雷克斯詹金斯博士的聯絡方式給我們的機構。

相關單字、片語

forward [ˋfɔrwəd]	向前；向將來；今後
company [ˋkʌmpənɪ]	公司，商號
project [prəˋdʒɛkt]	計畫；企劃
contact [ˋkɑntækt]	交往；聯繫，聯絡
kindly [ˋkaɪndlɪ]	勞駕，請；令人愉快地；讚許地；衷心地

organization [ˌɔrgənəˋzeʃən]	組織，機構，團體
client [ˋklaɪənt]	委託人，（律師等的） 當事人；顧客，客戶

9.3 出席會議

會話實例

A Would you be free for a meeting later today?

你今天晚點有空開會嗎？

B Let me check my agenda and get right back to you.

我看一下我的行程，馬上回覆你。

A We need to examine our financial position.

我們需要檢視財務狀況。

B Sure.

好的。

A Shall we say at around 15:00 in my office?

我們大約下午三點在我辦公室開會如何？

B Approximately, how long will it take? I have another meeting at 16:30.

大約會開多久？我四點半還有另個會議。

A I estimate that the meeting will take 30 minutes.

我估計會花半小時。

B Ok. I'll see you at 15:00 then.

好的，那到時三點見。

延伸例句

▶ I will attend a conference in Amsterdam next week.

我下禮拜會去阿姆斯特丹參加一個會議。

▶ I'm sorry that I couldn't attend the meeting.

很抱歉我無法出席會議。

▶ I would like to call a meeting to discuss our annual plan.

我想要召開會議討論我們的年度計畫。

▶ I'd like to arrange a meeting to discuss our strategy.

我想要召開會議討論我們的策略。

▶ The boss has called a meeting to discuss the discrepancies in the latest budget report.

老闆召開會議討論最近的預算報告的差異。

▶ Please confirm your attendance.
請確認是否出席。

▶ Please let me know a convenient place and time to meet.
請讓我知道你方便開會的地點及時間。

▶ I'm afraid I can't meet on May 3 at 14:00.
我恐怕無法在五月三號下午兩點與您會面。

▶ Let's start the meeting.
我們開始開會吧。

▶ May I have your attention please!
請大家注意！

▶ Here is the list of the attendees of this meeting.
這次這次會議參加者的名單。

▶ May is going to take the minutes.
梅會做會議紀錄。

▶ Joseph was told to keep the minutes at the conference.
約瑟夫被告知在會議上負責做紀錄。

▶ The agenda is as follows.
議程如下。

▶ We've come up with a great solution.
我們想出了一個很好的解決方案。

▶ I'm busy right now. I'm in a meeting.
我現在在忙，正在開會中。

▶ Thank you for coming.
謝謝你們的到來。

▶ Thank you for joining.
感謝您的加入。

相關 單字、片語

examine [ɪgˋzæmɪn]	檢查；細查；診察；審問；盤問
financial [faɪˋnænʃəl]	財政的；金融的
position [pəˋzɪʃən]	形勢，境況
approximately [əˋprɑksəmɪtlɪ]	大概；近乎
estimate [ˋɛstəmet]	估計，估量
conference [ˋkɑnfərəns]	正式）會議；討論會，協商會
discuss [dɪˋskʌs]	討論，商談；論述，詳述
strategy [ˋstrætədʒɪ]	策略，計謀；對策
boss [bɔs]	老板；上司
discrepancy [dɪˋskrɛpənsɪ]	不一致，不符，差異；不一致之處
latest [ˋletɪst]	最新的；最近的；最遲的
budget [ˋbʌdʒɪt]	預算；預算費；生活費，經費
report [rɪˋport]	報告
attendance [əˋtɛndəns]	到場；出席
convenient [kənˋvinjənt]	合宜的；方便的；便利的

afraid [ə`fred]	害怕的，怕的
attention [ə`tɛnʃən]	注意；注意力
attendee [ə`tɛndi]	出席者；在場者
minute [`mɪnɪt]	將……記入會議；記錄會議記錄
agenda [ə`dʒɛndə]	待議諸事項；議程；日常工作事項
solution [sə`luʃən]	解答；解決（辦法）

9.4 請求幫忙

會話實例

A Hey, Jill, are you in the middle of something?

嘿，吉兒，你正在忙嗎？

B Hey. I'm working on the upcoming project. How may I help you?

嘿，我正在忙接下來的這個專案。你需要幫忙嗎？

A Would you do me a favor when you're done, please?

可以請你忙完後幫我一個忙嗎？

B Yea, sure. Bring it on.

好，當然可以，說吧。

A I'd like to ask you to review the proposal for me.

我想要請你幫我複審提案。

B Ok. I'll let you know once I finish the task.

好，任務處理完了我會馬上通知你。

A Thank you!

謝啦！

延伸例句

▶ I was in the middle of a meeting.

我當時正在開會。

▶ Sorry, I have a few things coming up right now.

抱歉，我現在手上有些事要忙。

▶ I'm not available to talk right now. I'll call you back later.

我現在不方便說話。我稍後會回電。

▶ I'll get back to you later, is that okay?

晚點再回覆你可以嗎？

▶ Is there anything I can do to help you?

有什麼我能幫你的嗎？

▶ Can I help you with anything?
　有任何事情可以幫你嗎？

▶ Can I help you out?
　我可以幫你嗎？

▶ Do you need a hand?
　你需要幫忙嗎？

▶ Is there anything I can do to help?
　我能做任何事情幫忙嗎？

▶ Do you need anything from me?
　你需要我做任何事情嗎？

▶ Would you do me a favor, please?
　可以請你幫我一個忙嗎？

▶ Can you give me a hand?
　可以幫我一個忙嗎？

▶ Would you do me a favor and make a photocopy
　of this document for me?
　可以請你幫我複印這份文件嗎？

▶ Could I trouble you to go pick up the parcel?
　可以麻煩你去領包裹嗎？

▶ Could I bother you to send me the file?
　可以麻煩你將資料檔傳給我嗎？

▶ Could you kindly help me confirm the following information?

　能麻煩你協助我確認以下資訊嗎？

相關單字、片語

review [rɪ`vju]	再檢查，重新探討；複審； 批評，評論
proposal [prə`pozl]	建議，提議；計畫；提案
task [tæsk]	任務；工作；作業
trouble [`trʌbl]	麻煩
file [faɪl]	檔案，案卷，卷宗

⌂ track 85

9.5　升職加薪

會話實例

🅐 I'm so happy today!

　我今天好開心！

🅑 What? Got promoted?

　怎了？你升職了？

A Yea, I'm a senior director now.
對，我在是資深主任了。

B Wow! Congratulations!
哇！恭喜！

A Thanks a lot!
謝啦！

B Great job! Tommy! When do you take over the new position?
做得好！湯米！你什麼時候上任新工作？

A Next month. The job will come with management responsibilities, I hope I can do this.
下個月，這份工作會有更多管理責任，我希望能勝任。

B You will do great!
你會做得很好的！

延伸例句

▶ I just heard you got the senior manager job. Congratulations on the new position.
我剛得知你取得高階經理這個職位，恭喜你得到新的職位。

▶ Congratulations on your recent promotion.
恭喜你最近升職。

▶ Congratulations! You got promoted!
恭喜！你升職了！

▶ You have made a great contribution to the presentation. Congratulations on getting this contract.
你為這次的匯報貢獻良多，恭喜你得到這次的合約。

▶ His hard work has gained the recognition of the boss.
他的工作表現獲得了老闆的賞識。

▶ I got a raise today.
我今天被加薪了！

▶ I hope we will get both a higher bonus and higher pay.
我希望我們會有更高的獎金和薪水。

▶ It's payday.
今天是發薪日。

▶ It's my treat. I got a bigger bonus this month.
我請客，我這個月獎金比較多。

相關單字、片語

promote [prə`mot]	晉升
director [də`rɛktə]	主管；署長；局長；處長；主任；董事；經理

management [ˋmænɪdʒmənt]	管理；經營；處理
responsibility [rɪ͵spɑnsəˋbɪlətɪ]	責任
recent [ˋrisnt]	新近的，最近的；近來的；近代的
contribution [͵kɑntrəˋbjuʃən]	貢獻
presentation [͵prizɛnˋteʃən]	顯示，呈現；表現；描述
contract [kənˋtrækt]	契約；合同
gain [gen]	得到；獲得
recognition [͵rɛkəgˋnɪʃən]	承認；確認；認可
raise [rez]	加薪；加薪額
bonus [ˋbonəs]	獎金；額外津貼；特別補助
payday [ˋpe͵de]	支付日；發薪日；交割日

track 86

9.6 辦公室文具

會話實例

Ⓐ Good morning, this is Sunshine stationery company. How may I help you?

早安，這裡是陽光文具公司，需要幫忙嗎？

B Hello, this is Alison from Aeon film company. I'd like to order some office supplies.

哈囉，我是萬古電影公司的艾莉森，我想要訂辦公室用品。

A Ok. What would you like to order?

好的，你要訂什麼呢？

B I'd like five HP 63 black ink cartridges, a box of A4 paper and 40 file folders.

我想要五個惠普63的黑色墨水匣、一箱A4紙跟四十個檔案夾。

A Anything else?

還要別的東西嗎？

B Oh, and ten markers in black! Our address is 45, Long street.

噢，我還要十隻黑色馬克筆！我們的地址是長街四十五號。

A Okay, we'll deliver the supplies by 5 p. m. in the afternoon.

好的，我們會將用品在今天下午五點前送達。

B Thank you very much!

非常感謝！

延伸例句

▶ I'd like to order stationery and office supplies.
我想要訂購文具及辦公室用品。

▶ We need to order staples.
我們要預訂訂書針。

▶ How many sheets are there in one box?
一盒有多少張？

▶ We ran out of correction tapes.
我們沒有修正帶了。

▶ The new paper cutter is very sharp.
新的裁紙器很利。

▶ Can I borrow your calculator?
我可以跟你借計算機嗎？

▶ The shredder turned off and stopped working.
碎紙機壞掉了並停止運作。

▶ What colors of highlighter would you like?
你想要什麼顏色的螢光筆？

▶ Would you like them delivered to your desk or would you like to pick them up here?
你要我們送到貴公司櫃檯呢？還是你要來取貨？

⑨ 辦公室篇

相關單字、片語

stationery [`steʃənˌɛrɪ]	文具;信紙
aeon [`iən]	永世;萬古
supply [sə`plaɪ]	供給,供應
ink [ɪŋk]	墨水;油墨;墨汁
cartridge [`kɑrtrɪdʒ]	墨水筒,筆芯
paper [`pepɚ]	紙
folder [`foldɚ]	文件夾,文書夾,紙夾
marker [mɑrkɚ]	記號筆,馬克筆
staple [`step!]	釘書針
sheet [ʃit]	(紙等的)一張,薄板,薄片
correction [kə`rɛkʃən]	訂正,修改;校正
tape [tep]	膠布;透明膠紙;絕緣膠布
cutter [`kʌtɚ]	刀具;切割機;裁剪機
sharp [ʃɑrp]	鋒利的;尖的
calculator [`kælkjəˌletɚ]	計算機
highlighter [`haɪˌlaɪtɚ]	螢光筆
desk [dɛsk]	書桌;辦公桌;寫字臺;櫃臺;服務臺

9.7 職業、職位

會話實例

A Hello, I'm Peter. Welcome to the company!
哈囉，我是彼得，歡迎來到這家公司！

B Thank you. I'm Kevin. Nice to meet you.
謝謝，我是凱文，很高興認識你。

A What department do you work in?
你在哪個部門工作？

B I'm in the accounting department. What about you?
我在會計部門，你呢？

A I'm in the logistics department.
我在物流部門。

B How long have you been working here for?
你在這邊工作多久了？

A 7 years. Let me show you around.
七年，我帶你到處看看。

B Sure! Thank you.
好！謝謝你。

9 辦公室篇

延伸例句

▶ What do you do?
你從事什麼工作？

▶ What do you do for a living?
你從事什麼工作？

▶ What is your occupation?
你的職業是什麼？

▶ I'm a geography teacher.
我是地理老師。

▶ I work in banking.
我在銀行業。

▶ I work as a software developer.
我是軟體開發者。

▶ I'm responsible for developing new software apps for our smartphones.
我負責開發新的智慧型手機應用軟體。

▶ I manage the sales team.
我管理銷售組。

▶ This is my manager, Ben.
這是我的經理，班。

▶ Kathy, meet my supervisor Jason.
凱西，這是我的主管傑森。

▶ Let me introduce you to our sales manager, Tony Cooper.
為您介紹我們的業務經理東尼庫柏。

▶ I'd like you to meet our chief accountant, Sarah Miller.
為您介紹我們會計長莎拉米勒。

相關 單字、片語

accounting [ə`kauntɪŋ]	會計；會計學；結帳
logistics [lo`dʒɪstɪks]	後勤學；物流，運籌
living [`lɪvɪŋ]	生計；生活
occupation [ˌɑkjə`peʃən]	工作，職業
geography [`dʒɪ`ɑgrəfɪ]	地理學；地形；地勢
banking [`bæŋkɪŋ]	銀行業務；銀行業
software [`sɔft.wɛr]	軟體
developer [dɪ`vɛləpər]	開發者
sales [selz]	售貨的；銷售的
supervisor [ˌsupər`vaɪzər]	監督人；管理人；指導者
introduce [ˌɪntrə`djus]	介紹，引見
accountant [ə`kauntənt]	會計師；會計人員

10

就醫篇

🎧 track 88

10.1 藥局

會話實例

Ⓐ Hi, How can I help you?

嗨，需要幫忙嗎？

Ⓑ I have a bad headache. Do you have anything for headaches?

我頭好痛，你們有任何頭痛藥嗎？

Ⓐ Yes, I have a few choices.

有，我有幾種不同選擇。

Ⓑ My head has been aching since last night. What do you recommend?

我的頭從昨晚就開始痛了。你推薦哪一個？

Ⓐ I recommend this pain-killer. It has few side effects and you won't feel drowsy after taking it.

我推薦這個止痛藥，副作用很少，而且吃了不會嗜睡。

Ⓑ Ok, How much does it cost?

好，要多少錢？

A A pack of 20 is 5 U.S. dollars.

一盒20顆，五塊美金。

B I'll take it.

我買這個。

延伸例句

▶ I'm looking for a gargle.

我在找藥用漱口水。

▶ Do you have band-aids?

你有賣OK繃嗎？

▶ Are there any side effects?

吃了會有副作用嗎？

▶ How long does it take for the medicine to kick in?

要多久藥效才會生效？

▶ This cold medicine can ease your symptoms.

這款感冒藥可以緩解你的症狀。

▶ How many pills should I take a day?

我一天該吃幾顆藥？

▶ When should I take them?

什麼時候吃？

▶ Take two tablets twice a day.

一天吃兩片藥。

► Take one capsule with food.
和著食物一起服用一個膠囊。

► you should not take the medication on an empty stomach.
你不應該空腹服用此藥物。

► The pharmacist told me to take two tablets after every meal.
醫生告訴我每頓飯後服兩片藥。

相關單字、片語

ache [ek]	（持續性地）疼痛
drowsy [ˋdrauzɪ]	昏昏欲睡的；困倦的
gargle [ˋgɑrgl]	漱口；漱口藥
side [saɪd]	次要的；附帶的；從屬的
cffcct [ɪˋfɛkt]	效果，效力；作用；影響
medicine [ˋmɛdəsn]	藥，內服藥
kick in	開始運轉；開始生效
kick [kɪk]	踢
ease [iz]	減輕，緩和
pill [pɪl]	藥丸，藥片
tablet [ˋtæblɪt]	藥片
capsule [ˋkæpsl]	膠囊
empty [ˋɛmptɪ]	空的；未佔用的
stomach [ˋstʌmək]	胃
pharmacist [ˋfɑrməsɪst]	製藥者；藥劑師；藥商

10 就醫篇

10.2 看牙齒

會話實例

A Hello, I'd like to make an appointment to see the dentist.

哈囉，我想要預約看牙醫。

B May I have your name, please?

請問您的大名？

A My name is Jay Collins.

我叫傑柯林斯。

B What time are you available?

您什麼時候方便過來？

A Is tomorrow at 7 p.m. ok?

請問明天晚上七點可以嗎？

B Yes, we're available. What services are you going to do?

可以，你要做什麼服務呢？

A I'd like to do a dental check-up.

我想要做牙齒檢查。

B Alright, see you tomorrow evening.

好的，明天晚上見。

延伸例句

▶ My tooth hurts.
我的牙齒痛。

▶ I have a toothache.
我牙痛。

▶ I have an appointment with a dentist.
我有預約看牙醫。

▶ My gums are swollen.
我牙齦腫脹。

▶ It hurts when I chew.
我咬東西時會痛。

▶ I think I have a cavity in my teeth.
我想我可能有蛀牙。

▶ I feel pain when I eat something cold.
我吃冷的東西會痛。

▶ My gums bleed when I brush my teeth.
我刷牙時牙齦會流血。

▶ I just had my wisdom tooth pulled.
我剛去拔智齒。

▶ My dad is going to get an implant.
我爸爸要去植牙。

► The old man has terrible breath.
這位老先生有口臭。

► I would like a teeth cleaning and teeth whitening, please.
我想要洗牙跟牙齒美白。

► I use dental floss and mouthwash to keep my teeth healthy every day.
我每天用牙線和漱口水保持牙齒健康。

相關單字、片語

dentist [ˋdɛntɪst]	牙科醫生，牙醫
dental [ˋdɛnt!]	牙齒的；牙科的
tooth [tuθ]	牙齒；齒狀物
toothache [ˋtuθ͵ek]	牙痛
gum [gʌm]	齒齦，牙床
swollen [ˋswolən]	膨脹的；浮腫的
chew [tʃu]	嚼，咀嚼
cavity [ˋkævətɪ]	（牙的）蛀洞
teeth [tiθ]	tooth的名詞複數
pain [pen]	痛，疼痛
bleed [blid]	出血，流血
brush [brʌʃ]	刷
wisdom [ˋwɪzdəm]	智慧，才智，明智
pull [pʊl]	拉，拖，牽，拽；拔
implant [ɪmˋplænt]	植入物；植入管

whitening [ˋhwaɪtnɪŋ]	變白;塗白
floss [flɔs]	用牙線潔牙
mouthwash [ˋmaʊθ͵waʃ]	漱口藥,洗口藥
healthy [ˋhɛlθɪ]	健康的;健全的;有益於 健康的

 track 90

10.3 探病

會話實例

Ⓐ How are you feeling?
你感覺如何?

Ⓑ I'm getting so much better, thank you for coming.
我復原很多了,謝謝你過來。

Ⓐ Are you comfortable here?
在這還舒服嗎?

Ⓑ Yes, it's quiet and clean.
嗯,這裡很安靜又乾淨。

Ⓐ That's good. When will you be discharged?
那就好,你什麼時候會出院?

B I'll be discharged from the hospital in three days!

我再三天就可以出院了！

A I'll take you to your favorite restaurant!

我會帶你去你最愛的餐廳！

B I can wait!

我等不及了！

延伸例句

▶ How are you doing so far?

你目前康復情形如何？

▶ When is the visiting hour?

探病時間是什麼時候？

▶ Is there anything I can do for you?

我可以幫你做些什麼嗎？

▶ Do you want me to stay here with you tonight?

你要我今晚在這裡陪你嗎？

▶ Are you able to walk without assistance?

你自己可以走路嗎？

▶ I hope you get well soon.

祝你早日康復。

相關 單字、片語

discharge [dɪs`tʃɑrdʒ]	允許……離開；釋放
hospital [`hɑspɪt!]	醫院

永續圖書
線上購物網

www.foreverbooks.com.tw

旅遊英文一點通

雅致風靡　典藏文化

親愛的顧客您好，感謝您購買這本書。即日起，填寫讀者回函卡寄回至本公司，我們每月將抽出一百名回函讀者，寄出精美禮物並享有生日當月購書優惠！想知道更多更即時的消息，歡迎加入"永續圖書粉絲團"您也可以選擇傳真、掃描或用本公司準備的免郵回函寄回，謝謝。

傳真電話：（02）8647-3660　　　　　電子信箱：yungjiuh@ms45.hinet.net

姓名：		性別：	□男　□女
出生日期：　年　　月　　日		電話：	
學歷：		職業：	
E-mail：			
地址：□□□			
從何處購買此書：		購買金額：	元
購買本書動機：□封面 □書名 □排版 □內容 □作者 □偶然衝動			
你對本書的意見： 內容：□滿意□尚可□待改進　　編輯：□滿意□尚可□待改進 封面：□滿意□尚可□待改進　　定價：□滿意□尚可□待改進			
其他建議：			

總經銷：永續圖書有限公司

永續圖書線上購物網
www.foreverbooks.com.tw

您可以使用以下方式將回函寄回。

您的回覆，是我們進步的最大動力，謝謝。

① 使用本公司準備的免郵回函寄回。

② 傳真電話：（02）8647-3660

③ 掃描圖檔寄到電子信箱：

　　yungjiuh@ms45.hinet.net

沿此線對折後寄回，謝謝。

廣 告 回 信
基隆郵局登記證
基隆廣字第056號

2 2 1 0 3

 雅典文化事業有限公司　收
新北市汐止區大同路三段194號9樓之1

雅致風靡　典藏文化